TENDERFOOT TRAIL BOSS

Jack Brogan, the restless younger son of rancher Clint Brogan, was about to become engaged to Dawn Miller when the family learned that Jack's dominating older brother, Roary, was returning from a successful spell in the army. So as not to be eclipsed by Roary, Jack unexpectedly decided to take a Circle B herd to Kansas. But his problems started at once. Finally, ambushers robbed him of the payroll cash, and drove him to side with bank robbers — until his fortunes changed . . .

Books by David Bingley
in the Linford Western Library:

THE BEAUCLERC BRAND
ROGUE'S REMITTANCE
STOLEN STAR
BRIGAND'S BOUNTY
TROUBLESHOOTER ON TRIAL
GREENHORN GORGE
RUSTLER'S MOON
SUNSET SHOWDOWN

DAVID BINGLEY

TENDERFOOT TRAIL BOSS

Complete and Unabridged

LINFORD
Leicester

First published in Great Britain in 1983

First Linford Edition
published 2004

British Library CIP Data

Bingley, David, *1920 –*
    Tenderfoot trail boss.—Large print ed.—
Linford western library
1. Western stories
2. Large type books
I. Title II. Chatham, Larry, *1920 –*
823.9′14 [F]

ISBN 1–84395–260–2

Published by
F. A. Thorpe (Publishing)
Anstey, Leicestershire

Set by Words & Graphics Ltd.
Anstey, Leicestershire
Printed and bound in Great Britain by
T. J. International Ltd., Padstow, Cornwall

This book is printed on acid-free paper

1

At ten o'clock on a Saturday evening late in the month of March, several score of merrymakers were enjoying themselves in San Antonio's Community Centre, located in the uptown section of Second Street. At one time, the Centre had been a saloon with hotel facilities, but because it happened to be among stylish residences a group of well heeled local dignitaries had ensured that the saloon failed as a business enterprise. Its handsome lady proprietor, a former actress from the east coast, had been encouraged to set up business on Main. This she had done, and ever since she had prospered.

Since then the Centre had been run as a place of entertainment for long term town dwellers. The bills for its upkeep had been met by two ranchers, Clint Brogan of the Circle B and his old friend, Bert Miller, owner of the Box M.

Rumour had put it around that the Brogans were footing the bill for this particular shindig and, as Clint was in an expansive mood, no one had any reason to query the speculation.

The music makers, three violinists, a pianist and a drummer, were drinking beer during the first interval when the Millers' eligible, pretty daughter, Dawn, sidled through the standing guests and plumped herself down between her parents, Bert and Mary, on one of the two settees located in the secluded alcove reserved for the top brass.

Dawn was a shapely girl, dressed on this occasion in a bottle-green velvet dress with short flounced sleeves. Her long auburn hair, parted in the middle, swept around her freckled shoulders and concealed some of her exposed flesh which her mother thought would have been better covered.

Mrs Miller, plump and greying, in a

pale blue outfit, eased sideways to accommodate her restless daughter.

'Why, daughter, I do believe you've allowed dear Jack to get away from you, at last! Where in the world has he put himself? I can't see him anywhere around!'

Bert chuckled through cigar smoke. In a voice which Clint and Martha Brogan could easily hear, he remarked: 'There's one thing about the Brogans' second son, he doesn't ever let the grass grow under his feet. I guess he's lookin' over those Wilson girls, newly moved in along the creek. That's where I'd be if I was *his* age an' had the chance to slip away.'

Mrs Miller drew herself up as though she had been outraged. On the other settee, Martha Brogan blushed, while her husband, Clint — a big man with iron grey hair and straight black brows — gave out with his loud booming laugh, shaking his shoulders under his well-cut dark jacket.

Dawn merely shrugged and smiled.

She glanced in the direction of the couples standing about on the floor, failed to detect Jack who had danced with her consistently for forty minutes, and managed an unaffected pearl-toothed smile.

'Oh, shucks, Ma, why take on so? Me, I had to go to the ladies room. I'm sure gentlemen have to do something similar from time to time!'

Again, the two men laughed. A becoming blush was suffusing Dawn's long shapely neck when the drummer did a roll on his instruments and the mounting murmur of idle chatter was suddenly reduced.

'Ladies an' gentlemen, take your partners for the next dance. When you hear the music you won't need any further explanation, or introduction. Here we go now.'

The fiddlers played a chord standing up. Dawn stood up and moved through the waiting couples. She had no particular purpose in mind, but there were one or two young fellows she did not want to dance with. At the foot of the wide staircase which came down from the upper gallery, a farmer's son with big feet and huge hands bravely barred her way.

Good manners made the girl pause. She had almost made up her mind to dance with the fellow when a swift diversion occurred. Jack Brogan, the elusive young man, erupted into the action by sliding down the full length of the banister rail and dropping with great agility just between them. In fact, the would-be dancer had his left foot firmly trampled before Jack adjusted his balance and stepped off him.

Adjusting his string tie, and squaring his black jacket over his shoulders, Jack half-bowed to Dawn, smiled broadly and nodded to his rival. 'Sorry to keep you waitin', Sun-up. I got myself involved in a bit of private business on the top floor. Here we go!'

As the band began a lively reel, Jack swung Dawn clear of the other fellow and moved her into a convenient gap.

Dawn remarked: 'Restlessness will be your downfall. Booze, women or gambling?'

'Eh? What's that you say, girl?'

She gave him a close, green-eyed glare. 'What have you been up to?'

Jack's lean, cleanshaven face slowly relaxed. He let go of Dawn's right hand for a moment, gently finger-combed his well brushed brown hair, and gave her his most devastating smile. The look in her eyes suggested that the reddish highlights near his scalp were showing to good effect.

'While we were dancin', earlier, I got to thinkin' about how those rooms on the top floor were utilised before your pa an' mine took over the buildin'. So, I did a tour of the top floor, purely out of curiosity.'

Moving a little closer, Dawn asked: 'Did you find anything truly interesting in the private rooms?'

'Nothing I'd want to talk about to an eligible young woman. Er, no, not really.'

'Jack, do you realise that half this town expects the two of us to announce our engagement one of these days?'

He replied nonchalantly: 'Yes, I suppose they do, but there isn't any need to rush things, is there, amigo?'

Dawn was smart, well educated, good looking and she had plenty of personality, but Jack was privately thinking about what she had mentioned earlier. Namely, booze, women and gambling.

'No, I guess not, but there's lots of other young men who wouldn't keep me waiting, Jack. You're always duckin' out on things. And besides, an engagement need not be a short affair!'

Jack hastily glanced around him, wondering if any of the other dancers had heard the exchanges between them, but no one had. There was an air of speculation furrowing his brow as he danced on manfully, piloting his lissom partner first this way and then that.

'Jack? Did you hear what I said? Why are we moving towards the door? You ain't plannin' on dumpin' me again, are you?'

Dawn could talk as broadly as any waddie on her father's pay roll when she was in the mood.

'Yer, yer, I heard what you said, Sun-up. No, I didn't intend to dump you. That wasn't in my mind, at all. Only I have to go out of doors for a short spell. I want to think an' the grey matter won't work in this atmosphere!'

In a pirouetting turn, Dawn pressed herself against him.

'All right, the door it is. We'll both step out together. For a spot of fresh air. You know, sometimes you have the right ideas, Jack. Lead the way, but not too fast. We don't want to start improper rumours, do we?'

Out on the broad front sidewalk, there was a cool breeze, and the sounds of music were muted. Jack stepped up and down, briskly, holding Dawn tightly by the hand. Presently, he slipped out of his jacket and hung it around her shoulders. She said nothing, but her every movement seemed to blend in with his own. He stopped, and pointed.

'Say, who does that saddled bronc belong to, Sun-up? You're good at knowin' such things. Who do you figure would have it out in the street at this hour, ready for a quick move?'

Dawn shrugged her shoulders in the borrowed jacket. 'Well, as it happens, I'm familiar with that sorrel. It happens to be the property of Uncle Matt, but what it has to do with our little problem I can't think!'

'Can't you see I want to borrow it, Sun-up? Once round the town perimeter is all. Then I'll feel fresh an' I can think over this long term engagement you spoke of. What do you say? Matt ain't aimin' to leave town in a hurry, is he? An' it ain't as if we don't know each other, either.'

'I guess Matt's been held up some place, card playin' or something. Shucks, you could borrow the sorrel. But you don't go off ridin' without me!'

Side by side, they went down to hitchrail level. Jack untied the reins, but he was still stunned at the thought of Dawn riding double with him in her dance hall finery.

'Hell's bells, Sun-up. Dawn, that is. You can't go ridin' up behind me in that velvet outfit. Can you?'

Dawn flashed him her bewitching smile and shook her head. 'No, I don't think so. But if I happened to be in the saddle, an' you rode behind me an' manipulated the reins, all might be well. Don't you think so?'

Jack blinked, shrugged and urged himself towards agreement. Boosting a beautiful girl into a saddle ordinarily was quite something, but when she was in a long gown and dancing pumps, that was something else. The willing sorrel soon settled down to a steady walk, as Jack steered it out to the west of town and then all the way round the north end. On the way back, the young man slowed down their mount even more and Dawn leaned her back into him.

'By now you'll have realised that bein' engaged in the long term to me is no sort of hardship. An' even if it was, you could always make a run for the Mexican border — '

'Quit teasin' me, will you, Sun-up, I'm tryin' to think up a speech for when we get back. Right now, I've forgotten what it was I wanted to say.'

Dawn squirmed in the saddle and contrived to kiss him on the mouth, but she said nothing, and in a few minutes the plodding sorrel turned back into Second Street at the opposite end from when they started.

As they approached the Centre once more, a man in overalls and a soft peaked cap crossed over an intersection and called after them. Jack identified the stooping figure of Nate Schulz, the veteran telegraph clerk.

'All right, all right,' Jack protested. 'So what is so darned important, Nate, that it can't wait till mornin'? Shucks, I'm kind of tied up at the moment. You could say I've reached a crisis in my life. Well, sort of. Huh?'

Dawn's squirming body so tantalised Jack that he was unable to ignore the repeated pleas of the breathless clerk, who came on after them. At length, the young Texan accepted that there had to be a delay. He stopped the sorrel, waited for Schulz to come up with them, and grudgingly showed a modicum of politeness to the older man.

'It's for your father, Mr Jack. From your brother, Roary. Right now he's in Rosenberg, maybe two days' ride from here. Mr Jack, I thought you'd like to be the one to break the news to your Pa. Besides, I didn't ought to have left my office unattended.'

Although disquieting thoughts of a different nature were coursing through Jack's brain, he nevertheless acknowledged the other's efforts.

'I know what you've done, Nate, an' you did right. Get back to your office. I'll see Pa gets the message, an' in the right fashion, too. I'll be along to settle up with you tomorrow. That do you?'

Schulz nodded, doffed his cap and thankfully retreated.

'Jack, is this goin' to make a difference?'

As he helped her to dismount, Jack dredged up a deep sigh. 'Sun-up, I want you to go on in, alone. Give me time to read the message. Five minutes, say? Then stop the band, and I'll be in there to make an announcement. That suit you? Okay. So, off you go.'

He patted her lightly on the bottom as she danced easily up the steps and crossed the boards of the sidewalk. Almost at once, he was alone. He felt like a man in a trance. In his hand, the signal pad fluttered, bringing him back to reality. His legs appeared to have gone heavy.

* * *

In the hall, Dawn dodged in and out of the dancers, waited impatiently for the Brogans and her mother and father to

13

retire from the dance and be seated again. People who sought to communicate with her received a short sharp smile, or a brief answer and presently, the four older people returned to the alcove just before the dance came to an end. They took time to flop down in their seats, but the girl waited for them to get comfortable before she attempted to get their attention. Mrs Miller opened her mouth to comment on certain unwanted marks on the daring dance dress, but Dawn forestalled her.

'Ma, everything's all right. In a minute, Jack is going to come indoors and make an announcement. Maybe two, if I know him. So will you settle yourselves down an' stop lookin' as if the world was comin' to an end?'

A saucy confident smile was enough to please Clint Brogan and her father, but the women were more intrigued and piling up in their minds quite a few possibilities. The oldest fiddler looked surprised when Dawn asked him to hold up the next dance, but he gave a

14

toothy grin when he heard why.

'Ladies an' gentlemen, young Mr Brogan, Mr Jack Brogan, that is, wants to make an announcement. So let's have a bit of quiet for young Jack B!'

Dawn moved off the dais to stand in front of it. The drummer played a heavy roll, the young couples all clapped and Jack came into view, moving slowly and with apparent reluctance. He brushed back his unparted hair, waved the message paper and bowed briefly.

'Ladies and gents, dear friends. Hope you didn't miss Dawn an' me when we went out for a breath of air. Our exit was timely, because Nate Schulz had a message for the Brogan family and we encountered him. I'm tellin' you all, as well as my dear parents that Roary, my brother, has just finished with the army. Right now, he is two days' ride east of San Antone an' he's comin' home for good!'

Clint Brogan rose to his feet with alacrity, clearly overjoyed to hear the family news. Dawn, meanwhile, reached up to Jack and clasped his free hand in both her own. The room filled with uproar, as friends of the Brogans acknowledged the return from the army of a son of the town, the son of a former mayor.

Dawn murmured: 'I'm really pleased for you, Jack!'

His expression, however, continued to be one of anguish. The young man fidgeted with his jacket, which seemed to be too small since Dawn had returned it to him. From the back of the hall, Clint prompted his son, who resumed.

'And that ain't all, folks. In recent years, my Pa has seen fit at times to encourage me into more responsible ways, as becomes the son of a prosperous rancher. Well, I want you to know that when the spring herd of beeves goes north from the Circle B, maybe as soon as tomorrow, *I'll* be with it!'

This time, the applause was warm, but less noisy. Dawn moved much closer, and hugged her man, although his announcement had left her stunned. It was not what she had expected to hear, at all.

Clint Brogan extended an arm, and pointed at his son. 'I hope you know what you're doin' young fellow!'

'Sure! Sure, Pa, I know what I'm doin'. I've thought it out! Don't bother your head. It'll work out all right, so help me, it will!'

The band leader looked askance. Jack nodded for him to announce the next dance, which he did. The musicians struck up and the melody had the feet going and the bodies swaying. Gradually, Jack became more and more aware of Dawn, and of the emotional state which had built up in her. As he lacked initiative, he grabbed her to him and swung her onto the dance floor.

'Jack, did you forget something? I appreciate the telegraph might have been a shock, but we were talkin' about something entirely different out there.'

'Sun-up, I'm sorry. Will you go along

with what I'm doin', what I've said? The announcement about the engagement can wait. I shan't be away all that long. You won't run off with anyone else. It'll be our secret. Just the two of us will know. How does that grab you?'

He examined the girl's face closely, but her reaction fell short of his expectations. Her green eyes were rounded, and she would have looked shocked, except for a certain wateriness which suggested tears were not far off.

* * *

That night, Clint and Martha Brogan and their friends, Bert and Mary Miller spent the night in the private upper rooms of the Centre.

By contrast, Jack Brogan absented himself from the gathering at an early hour. Dawn eventually retired into the room next to her parents. The Millers were surprised to hear that Jack had not been with her after the dance. The

Brogans also shared in their friends' mild concern, but it was concluded that Jack had collected his mount from the livery and gone out to the Circle B to start his preparations for his imminent departure north with the trail herd.

Before Martha Brogan fell asleep her thoughts made her restless.

'Clint, do you think Jack will go through with it? Going north with the beeves, I mean. Will he really make the effort this time?'

Clint was glad of the darkness to hide his troubled features. 'How do *I* know, wife? Tomorrow we'll know better. You, you ought to concentrate on your older son's arrival home from the army. That much is certain any how. As to Jack, we'll just have to wait an' see. However, if you want me to guess, I believe it is just about possible this time, on account of Roary bein' due. There's strong feelin' between our two boys. One is forthright, determined and capable, while the other is like a grasshopper. Even at the age of twenty-five. Sometimes I wish he'd been in the army like Roary. That sort of trainin' would have made him responsible for certain.'

Martha was silent for a while. Just when Clint thought she had gone to sleep, she murmured: 'Anyway, Jack is good with horses. Every bit as good as Roary. I hope he does the manly thing, although Dawn won't be pleased. When she came back into the Centre, earlier this evening I could have sworn she expected him to announce their engagement. If she did, he gave *her* a bigger shock than he gave us. Surely it will all turn out for the best. I sincerely hope so.'

A number of silent prayers were said touching on the same subject.

★　★　★

The eyes of ten men and three women were filled with interest when Dawn Miller rode up to the Brogan ranch house at ten o'clock the following morning, forking her own spritely grey mare.

There were faint grey smudges under her eyes, hinting that she had not slept very well but no one mentioned her appearance, although in her blue shirt, denims and grey flat-crowned hat she was a sight to see, especially for the men. Her ribboned pony's tail of auburn hair bobbed at the back of her neck as she nodded and smiled to Martha, busily tidying up a rancher's clutter from the boards of the front gallery.

'Good day to you, Dawn. Hope you slept well. Guess you want to talk with my men. Clint's in the smithy. Jack's away up range, exercisin' his horse an' helpin' with countin' the trail herd. Ain't no sign of our Roary arrivin' today. Maybe it'll be tomorrow. Him an' that buddy of his, Will Hobbs, they'll be celebratin' their release, I guess. Can I get you a cup of coffee?'

'No thanks, Mrs Brogan. I'll mosey into the smithy an' talk for a while with

Clint. That's if he can spare the time. You must be all excited, with one son goin' away an' the other one comin' home for good. My, my, this mare sure is restless.'

Presently, Dawn went off to the smithy. She left Martha wondering if Dawn and Jack had parted on good terms the previous evening.

Martha was still puzzled.

★ ★ ★

In the smithy, Ezekial, the ageing negro blacksmith, had just finished shoeing a restless chestnut which Clint had recently bought for his own use as a riding horse. As soon as Zeke noticed Miss Dawn, he straightened his broad muscular back, mopped off his glistening face and forehead and beamed. Clint, whose checkered shirt showed signs of perspiration in the heat to which he was not accustomed, also shared Zeke's pleasure.

'Why, Dawn! How nice to see you

here so early in the day! Especially since we were so late in getting to our beds. Are your mother and father all right?'

Dawn removed her hat, beamed at the pair of them and assured Clint that her folks had slept reasonably well, in town. After the girl had made the acquaintance of the youthful chestnut, the conversation moved around to the reason for her visit.

Clint tactfully dismissed Zeke, by instructing him to take the chestnut over to the corral before taking a coffee break in the bunkhouse.

'You're goin' to miss Jack when he goes north, Dawn, especially as you've been so close of late. For my money, it's time he settled down, but he seems to have made up his mind this time about goin' north with the herd. If he sees it through, the experience will be good for him, one way or another. I'd like to make it clear that I haven't been puttin' any undue pressure on him recently, though. The decision he came up with last evenin' was all his own doin'.

'Right now, he's up range involved in countin' the herd due for Kansas. Some time later in the day, he should be back here to have Zeke check over some of the men's ridin' horses. He'll surely be back, but I can't say when. Were you thinkin' of waitin' for him, Dawn?'

The girl shrugged and turned to look out of the window. 'I don't know, Clint. Somehow I don't think it would be wise. He's clearly very busy. If he wants to see me before he goes, then he'll make time to come over.' Dawn edged towards the door. 'Clint, would you think it interference on my part if I asked Uncle Matt to go along with Jack, as one of his team?'

A brief frown left the rancher's rugged features. He beamed. 'An excellent idea. One which I fully approve of. But we mustn't allow Jack to think he needs a lot of special back up. Sure, Matt Hansen will always be welcome on any trail drive from the Circle B in my time!'

'And long may that be, Clint,' Dawn

replied, with a shy giggle.

Clint took her by the arm and escorted her as far as the ranch house kitchen.

* * *

The huge pall of dust swinging down from the north made it absolutely clear to everyone involved around the Brogan ranch buildings that the horses of the remuda were not far away. Dawn Miller had left an hour earlier, and Martha and Clint were still a trifle nervous as their son Jack headed the eighty horses into the corral.

Clint hurried over to be the first to speak with his unpredictable son. Jack, however, still seemed determined to go with the herd. He was dusty, slightly out of sorts with himself and extremely thirsty, but the resolution was still there.

'A thousand and ten beeves at the count, Pa. Maybe ten or eleven of these broncs need attention before the day is out!'

'You missed Dawn by an hour, son. She came an' went, as we didn't know when you'd be back. Is that all right?'

Jack finished drinking from a canteen of cool water. 'I guess so, Pa. If anyone could turn me away from ramrodding the herd, it would be Sun-up. So, in a way, I'm glad I missed her.'

'You'll have thirty-five days in which to deliver the herd into the hands of Colonel Seth J. Baron at North Flats, in Kansas. He knows us. An old Texas man, as you know. If you keep to the time limit, he will pay you cash at twenty a head. Don't lose the money.'

Jack's expression turned mean. He was framing up to use harsh words to Clint, but his father spoke first.

'That payment will be yours. Enough to set you up independently. If you manage to claim the full payment from the Colonel, we'll then see whether you turn out to be a prodigal son, or a normal Brogan. Get my meanin' Jack?'

'You mean I'll gamble it all away, or come back dutifully home with the money, don't you?'

'I mean you'll either fritter it away, or lose it, or use it to some worthwhile purpose. Dawn will sure as hell be expectin' you back here with the herd money, but me, I'm not so sure. You may be my son, but I don't find it easy to read your thoughts.'

After a while, Jack grinned. 'It seems you like gamblin' as you know I do, Pa. We'll have to see, won't we? In the meantime, how about helpin' me to cut out the ponies which need Zeke's attention?'

'I'll do that right gladly, young man. Give Zeke a whistle, he's round the buildings somewhere.'

Presently, they were both coated in dust: so much so that Martha could not identify them without straining her eyes.

2

At five o'clock the following morning, the cookhouse of the Circle B was beginning to get into action. Juan Fuente, who usually cooked for the home crew, had elected to stack up the chuck wagon for this particular trip and leave his ranch chores to the youthful Ah Feng, his Chinese assistant.

Consequently, there was plenty to do on the cooking front, as well as preparing for the imminent depature of the drovers.

Jack Brogan partook of his breakfast in the bunkhouse so as not to disturb his mother and others in the main building who had the chance to sleep for an hour or so longer. Jack was still edgy and impatient. He had not this far contacted the regular trail boss, Rudy Backmann, who was a capable veteran with an uncertain temper and a background which no one locally knew much about. Rudy had been out on the town the previous day and had not returned to the spread within the customary hours. However, he had a reputation for returning late and apparently without sleep which did not seem to interfere with the pressing chores of getting a trail outfit on the move.

Felipe Fuente, Juan's youthful cousin, entered the bunkhouse shortly after the approach of a single horse had been heard. Jack drained the dregs of his second cup of coffee and scowled at the lean Mexican's poker face in an effort to guess the identity of the newcomer. Was it brother Roary? Or was it Backmann bent upon some futile irrelevant argument before the outfit got under way?

'Well, don't just stand there, Felipe! Who is it?'

Felipe's regular inscrutable features broke into a brief smile as he nodded. 'Senor Jack, you will be surprised. It is

Matt Hansen, and he says he has permission to join the trail outfit from your father. That's good news, isn't it? I asked him to come in because he doesn't look as if he was in his bed last night. Hope you didn't mind?'

Matt Hansen, a long term bachelor and the brother of Mary Miller, had remained something of a rolling stone since the days of the war between the north and south. Sometimes, he stayed in town to play cards or to work as a barman. Other times, he shared his undoubted skills with horses and cows between the Circle B and the Box M. Matt hitched the sorrel horse which Jack had borrowed outside the Community Centre and slouched into the bunkhouse with the whites of his grey eyes a distinct shade of pink and his battered Texas-rolled stetson pushed well to the back of his head and apparently resting on his biggish ears which protruded from the sides of his head.

Jack eyed him over critically. Matt's

legs appeared to be more bowed than of late. Although he was tired, a humorous quirk extended his thin mouth and the even thinner black line of hair which constituted his moustache.

'Well, if it ain't the newest Brogan trail boss, in the flesh. Your new hand reportin' for duty, mister. Thought you'd have been up with the herd by this hour, Jack. My, my, that coffee smells good to a man who's been up all night.'

'Welcome to the Brogan outfit, Matt. I don't need to ask what you've been doin' all night, do I? Gamblin' I reckon. It's good to have you along, amigo, but if you can imbibe an' eat quickly it'll please me 'cause I want to get to north range as soon as ever possible. Right?'

Juan produced a cup and filled it with black coffee for the newcomer.

'I take it you've talked to Rudy Backmann already? No? He ain't around. In that case, he's probably ridden straight on to the range. He left the card game in town a couple of hours before I did, havin' lost a fair bit of his funds, so he won't be in a good temper to start off with.'

Gradually, the latest information permeated the busy group of workers. Fifteen minutes later, Jack and the latest recruit headed north to join the herd, leaving others to supervise the chuck wagon and bring along the remuda.

★   ★   ★

Rudy Backmann was never an easy character to deal with. On this occasion, his big-barrelled plodding black gelding with its distinctive white blaze had carried him asleep on its back all the way from town to the north range where a sleepy night guard had halted the animal and assisted the trail boss to dismount.

As soon as he was properly awake, Rudy started to complain. Butch, the hirsute rider who had assisted him, stopped an unpleasant tirade about the chuck wagon not being on the range, the new boss not being there to welcome him and various other small niggling things.

When he searched through his pockets he found that his folding money had all been used up in his most recent gambling stint, except for ten dollars put back into his pocket by a generous winner. Matt Hansen, in fact. A man with connections, who could afford to lose and still be all right for credit in town.

Rudy swallowed a few mouthfuls of campfire coffee, but the state of his whitened tongue was not improved by the inferior liquid. Nor was his thirst. Nor was his temper.

He cast the dregs aside, and thumped his booted feet this way and that, occasionally glancing in the direction of the bawling cattle which were protected this far by Circle B range wire. His feet were hot in the boots, which had not been off his legs for many hours.

'Hey, Butch, come here a minute.

You, too, Lefty. You heard about the change of command at the top? You have. Well, I for one do not welcome it. Puttin' in the owner's shifty second son is not good for the business. I take it you'd agree to that?'

The two hands, Butch and Kramer, kept their tongues still while at the same time giving the impression that they agreed with their questioner. A slight breeze and the necessity to come up with something totally damning helped to clear the foreman's fuddled mind.

'So, the chuck wagon will not be long, even if young Brogan cries off. So you say. Now, tell me this. How many hands do we have to manhandle this one thousand head all the way to Kansas? How many? Come on now. List 'em off on your fingers, will you?'

Kramer demurred, but when Backmann started to lose his temper, the blond-haired German drover hastily complied. He had not wanted to do the counting on his fingers because he had lost one finger during a nasty encounter with a wild horse in a rodeo.

'Well, now, if you'll hold on a second, Rudy, I'll give it a try. There's Jack Brogan, yourself, the two Mexicans, Juan and Felipe. Then there's Dan. Dan Adler. An' Pete Rossi, an' Butch, here. Red Greaves, an' Charlie Brand. That's about all, I'd say!'

Backmann scowled. 'It ain't enough! You hear me?' He started to shout, and to repeat himself. And then it occurred to him that he did not not know the total, and his mind became fuddled again.

'Hey, Butch, you ain't bein' very helpful! How many does that make altogether?'

Fortunately, Butch Malone had taken a proper count at the outset.

'If I've counted right, that makes ten. An' if you don't believe me, count them yourself, 'cause you're supposed to be the hombre with the brains at this time of the morning.'

At times, it appeared that Backmann

was shouting at the beeves. Behind his back, some of the men already named were staring at two riders who were coming down the nearby slope from the direction of home buildings. As they were under close scrutiny from the riders and there was nothing wrong with their eyesight, they kept the peace, neglected to tell the angry foreman, and allowed the situation to develop.

'Hey, Rudy, I hope you ain't forgettin' me!' Matt Hansen's voice carried with ease. 'You were well under the influence when the two of us parted in the early hours. I wouldn't want you to get the count wrong at the outset. After all, if you can't count the hands in a trail crew accurately, you ain't goin' to be much good when it comes to countin' a thousand head of cattle, are you?'

Backmann left off shouting and turned to meet the new challenge. In the meantime, Matt — a past master in the art of handling himself in tricky situations — called out to several of the boys whom he knew by name and gradually got himself accepted into the group.

Jack was already in a bad temper, having heard quite a lot of the former trail boss' tirade. He dismounted with a show of lethargy, and only gave the men a short acknowledgement and a brief smile.

'Mornin' boys, sorry you ain't had the use of the chuck wagon this a.m., but it is on its way and should arrive within a half hour. Give yourselves a smoke, or something, why don't you? In a short while, you'll be tastin' the dust of the remuda, an' dust is something you'll come to know too well. Rudy! Mr Backmann, if you prefer it, I'd like a private word with you.'

Backmann turned to him and pointed a horny index finger at him.

'A conversation between the two of us is timely, *Mr* Brogan. We don't have enough hands to move one thousand head of restless beef all the way to Kansas without takin' risks!'

Jack allowed a short interval to elapse after the fiery man's utterance. 'I agree with you. You're right. All the same, we shall be startin' out with the men already mentioned to you. Anyone else we're fortunate enough to add to our startin' numbers will be acquired along the way! Is that all right by you?'

By agreeing with him, Jack had taken some of the strength out of the argument, but Backmann was determined on a showdown of sorts, and his mind scattered around for fuel to maintain his flow of words. He pulled off his stained broad flat stetson, rolled it under his arm to remove the excess of dust from it, replaced it over his receding fair hair. His full lips came and went as he pursed them and the seams in his leathery countenance seemed to protest.

'I'm glad you agree with me, Mr Brogan, but I want to tell you something you may not know, seein' as how you haven't ridden with a trail herd before. We ought to have three or four more hands right from the start, 'cause in some respects the first day or two are crucial. The herd has to be taught how to move, how to do as we want it to, on trail, an' that sure is mighty important in cow nursin'!'

'I agree with you again, but don't you think you're makin' a fool of yourself the first mornin' on the job? You ought to know yourself by now. Havin' lost your money gamblin' and then your sleep through bein' liquored. Any man of your experience with more sense would have been in his bunk nice an' early last night!'

'You're tryin' to pick a quarrel with me because I'm givin' you good advice an' you can't take it! How come you're here on this trail drive, anyways? What's gotten into you that you can't stay at home like other times an' clown around the town?'

Jack took in a deep breath and rested his gloved hands on his hips.

'Backmann, there are ranchers in this county won't employ you because you're such a bad tempered ornery cuss to deal with. Let me remind you, you're drawin' good Brogan money for what you do, but you're an employee, not the fellow who tells the owner how to run his show. So belt up. You've said enough already. You're settin' a bad example to the men, an' what's more they don't like it!'

Jack's voice had also risen. Backmann took a step forward and raised a fist. The bawling of the beeves seemed to grow louder in the ears of Jack Brogan. He stepped back half a pace, dropped his right handed Colt to the ground and shook his arms to loosen up the muscles.

'Brogan, you see here. Don't start puttin' my regular team of drovers against me! They do as I tell them, an' I tell them right!'

'If I'd known how they have to put up with your hellish bad temper you wouldn't be handling the Circle B brand at this time!'

Backmann also unshipped his hardware. He took a vicious swing at the younger man, who sidestepped his forward rush and hit him hard in the midriff. Backmann came up short, gasping for air and turning for the next exchange. Pure hatred lurked at the back of his hard blue eyes. Both men then swung and missed. Backmann lost his big hat, as fresh perspiration moistened his brow. Jack calmly took off his own and tossed it aside. Backmann advanced like a prize fighter, one foot well in advance of the other. This time he feinted with his right and immediately threw his left, but Jack's reflexes were fast. He casually stepped away from the other's arms, and took his eyes off the target. As soon as Backmann appeared to have done the same, the younger man moved in really fast and struck straight and hard with his left hand, drawing blood from a cut lip. Two swings from Backmann made Brogan shift hurriedly once again. One of them missed altogether, while the other merely brushed the side of his head.

As Backmann retreated to get his breath, Brogan followed him up, feinted with a right to the stomach and scored with a left to the side of the head.

A head down rush from Backmann bore Brogan back, but the latter managed to turn his heavier opponent and clip him hard on the side of his neck. Backmann head butted and Brogan clouted the back of his neck. After that, most of the exchanges went Brogan's way. The men crowded closer and began to shout for Jack, but he knew that too much of that partisanship at the outset would make his task more difficult in the future.

When lack of breath was reducing Backmann to a punching bag, Jack stepped away. 'All right, that's enough.'

Backmann made a sneak attack, but Jack sidestepped it and tripped him up. 'You hear me, men, Mr Backmann has challenged my authority at the first opportunity. He's backed up his challenge with fists, and lost. Maybe he's still worthy of his job as segundo on this run. We'll have to wait and see.'

Rudy picked himself up, dabbed his cuts on a soiled bandanna, and collected his discarded gun. A certain look in his eye made Jack wonder if he would ever use it against him.

'One thing, before I go back to speed up the wagon. If Backmann isn't satisfied to take orders from me, he can go back to the home ranch and stay there. I say this on my own authority. It's only fair. Bad blood is a poor basis for a trail drive.'

So saying, Jack dusted himself down, remounted his spritely chestnut gelding and rode back up the slope. Already, the distinctive sounds made by protesting mules was outdoing the bawling of beeves for volume.

Behind him, Backmann, who had lost face, sought to improve his image with the men. 'All right, Brogan, you've made your point!' he bellowed. 'An' this will surprise you, I will go back to the ranch an' stay there! You can stumble along the best way you know how with that herd of green beeves, but it won't be botherin' me, no sir. As if other ranchers would balk at hirin' me.'

He made a rude gesture at the diminishing back of his new master, and turned triumphantly, hoping to catch some of the hands grinning. None of them did. As the leading pair of mules came over the hill top Matt Hansen moved alongside of Backmann.

'Just between the two of us, Rudy, I think you made a wise decision there. That's exactly what I would have done. Go back to old man Brogan, an' take my chance with his number one son, Roary. The one who is due back from the army. Now, there's the sort of fellow to get along with. Newly promoted Lieutenant Roary Brogan, United States cavalry. He'll sure as hell put the home crew through their paces, yes, siree!'

While Matt stoked his tobacco pipe, Backmann's mind worked on the latest revelations. He accepted the makings from Butch Malone and staggered off to think over the situation.

Either he had not been told of the older son's return to the ranch, or the liquor he had consumed in the past twenty-four hours had wiped out the memory of his being told. Roary Brogan back on the ranch, full of new importance as an officer of the cavalry? The locality was all legend and rumour about the older Brogan boy's early exploits. Backmann did not fancy him at all. He began to wonder if he had been outmanoeuvred by this upstart member of the Brogan family, and how he could stay with the herd without considerable loss of face. It wasn't going to be easy, re-establishing himself in the eyes of Brogan, Hansen and the others. Somehow, though, he would have to try.

* * *

With mixed feelings about leaving in such a hurry, Jack, nevertheless, did all in his power to expedite the departure of the trail herd, and consequently the whole outfit was able to start out on trail before mid morning.

At the outset, Backmann and his original drovers were allowed to settle into a routine to get the beeves moving. At first, the beasts were in a querulous, fretful mood; however, the pace required of them was not excessive, and there were several small pools or lakes along the local route where they were able to slake their thirst without a lot of fuss. Furthermore, at that time of the year the land was lush with new green grass which was sprouting through all the time and making the food side of the beasts' needs very easy to deal with.

While Backmann and his regular drovers were dealing with the straggle of cattle, Jack Brogan, Felipe Fuente and Matt Hansen gave their attention to the remuda. One or two spare horses were hitched to the back of the chuck wagon. Having taken that precaution, it was easy to take the bulk of the riding stock away from the beeves and establish a better pace.

The midday halt on that first day was late in the afternoon. The drovers, except for the nightguards, therefore had a short working day. Having achieved eight miles on the initial day, the pace was stepped up on the second and third. Nine miles were accomplished on the second and just under eleven on the third.

Juan Fuente's drink and food back-up was very efficient, and still there was a feeling that the drovers were short-handed.

For the night camp on the third day, the remuda was quite close to the wagon and the camp fire. It was a time when the hatchet seemed to be buried between the top man and the segundo. Backmann had long since recovered from his hangover, and he chose that particular stop to further his argument that the outfit was undermanned.

As the off duty members of the crew strolled round the fire, exercising their legs and taking in more coffee, Backmann singled out Jack and engaged him in conversation.

'Jack, I regret the angry words and actions which occurred on the first morning. I'm still here, an' you've expressed yourself so far as being satisfied with the progress bein' made. If you'll listen to me, I'd like to put over my point about manpower.

'This far, there's been nothing at all to extend my boys, or to upset the beeves. First time we're put to the test, you'll see we are short on the ground. A couple of small accidents to my boys an' we would end up with large gaps along the perimeter of the herd. And that way, sooner or later, mistakes are made, and cattle are lost.'

As they strolled, Backmann fished around in his thoughts for words which would back up his argument. He was about to take his reasoning further when Jack suddenly replied.

'I think you know your job as a trail boss, Rudy. And you argue well when you stick to what you know, too. But where in tarnation are we to get three more hands to boost the team this side of the Brazos?'

For the first time since they began their discussion, it occurred to Backmann that Jack might be in sympathy with his point of view, and not talking simply to win an argument. He grinned broadly, whipped off his big hat and dusted it.

'Well now, Jack, that ain't such a big problem as you might think. We're well up in Edwards Plateau country right now. By tomorrow, we'll be real close to a small settlement which serves traders between the Pecos River to westward, and places like Houston an' Dallas to the east. Blackwood, it's called. Not very big on the map, but useful for travellers passin' through. If you like, I could take a short ride out to the station an' see if any of my old buddies are there and available for cattle drivin'.'

'All right, then. On your say-so, if they want work. You can absent yourself at mid-mornin' tomorrow an' rejoin us durin' the noon break.'

Jack emphasised the obvious terms under which extra helpers would be taken on, and then turned away to give his attention elsewhere. Matt Hansen, not far away in the background, raised his arched eyebrows in wonder and started to speculate about the outcome.

* * *

They came from the west the following day spread out in a line of three with Rudy Backmann perhaps five yards ahead of them.

All the regulars, from Juan Fuente to the sleepiest of the night guards, broke off from what they were doing and stared at them in great interest.

Backmann swung to the ground and threw the reins of his white-blazed gelding in the direction of Felipe. The latter was a fast eater, in any case, and a bit of extra work during his food break did not bother him at all. Felipe then shared his own interest between the three tough-looking newcomers and their equally mean-looking mounts.

'Jack, boys, I'd like to introduce these three hombres who've volunteered to join us up to Kansas,' Backmann began. 'Link. Link Thompson was more or less born in the saddle. You can tell Frenchy Dupont because he still wears a coonskin cap like he did when he lived in Canada. And Burro, Burro McNye. Well, he's the one with the hide jacket. You can guess for yourselves what animal it came from.'

Backmann went on talking, putting a name to all the Circle B men presented. By the time he had finished, he was showing signs of thirst and was glad to line up at the chuck wagon along with the men he had acquired.

As the recently arrived trio worked their way through fresh beef and biscuits, Felipe returned and began to hold an animated conversation in fast, elided Spanish with his kinsman in the wagon. It was as well that Juan, who was doing most of the listening, had a poker face.

Felipe was saying: 'Look at that Thompson. Behind his brown beard and moustache he carries a short upper lip over rabbit teeth. Enough to put any self-respecting *Mexicano* off his food for good. *Que raro*. Having all that hair on his face, the top of his head appears to be bald!

'Observe that one in the skin hat. A miniature Rocky Mountain grizzly, is he not? And the other, the one who is called Burro. I do not believe it is because he wears a burro hide jacket. It is because he has the long head and pointed ears of a mixed quadruped. What a trio! Fancy meeting them alone, on trail! I wonder if we shall have trouble with them on the journey. Our Rudy, he knows some strange men, *no*?'

'Time, *muchacho*,' Juan replied calmly. 'Time will tell!'

Shortly afterwards, Rudy Backmann became restless. He started to whistle off-key, and all the crew knew that he was anxious to get the herd on its feet again.

Thompson, Dupont and McNye all stayed closed to the main body of the herd. At the same time, Matt Hansen — acting on Jack's orders — kept them under observation as much as possible with the aid of an old spyglass.

3

There was thunder in the skies on the fourth night out, but soon after dawn the heavenly atmosphere appeared to have cleared. The drovers, all amateur weather forecasters, were inclined to believe that the day would pass off uneventfully, at least in regard to the weather.

Jack, Matt and Felipe broke out fresh horses from the rope corral and attached a few spares to the tailgate of the wagon, as was customary. One by one, the crew came in and collected their respective mounts. Thompson, Dupont and McNye, the three newcomers were among the last to collect and as they did so, the remuda crew kept a sharp eye on them.

'Well, Matt, what do you make of our new two-legged assistants?' Jack asked drily.

Matt shrugged. 'I kept the glass on them for an hour or two yesterday afternoon, but when Rudy shifted 'em over to the right flank there was too much dust to study the way they were behavin'. This far, I haven't seen anythin' particularly suspicious, but just the same I have this gut feelin' they're workin' for themselves, not for the Brogan outfit.'

Jack turned to Felipe. 'You exchanged a few ideas with Juan over them yesterday, Felipe. Do you have any suspicions?'

'Lots of suspicions, but only suspicions, Senor Jack. Perhaps it would be smart to do a number check at the first suitable opportunity, eh?'

Matt, who had worked this section of Texas many times before, thought Felipe had come up with a good idea. 'I believe there's a defile up ahead, just a mile or two. If we could go through with the remuda before the beeves arrive, I could hide myself wide of the defile an' do a secret count.

How would that be?'

'I'm glad you came along, Matt. How's your arithmetic?'

'Not at all bad, amigo. I use a knotted rope for high figure countin'. One knot for every hundred animals. Let's get a move on, if that's what you have in mind!'

The weaving herd put up a lot of dust at first and, in trying to outmanoeuvre the drovers riding at point, Matt allowed the horses to get too close to the beeves for a while, but as the low land snaked out ahead, meandering incessantly; the keepers of the horse outfit gradually worked their charges further away.

Jack, riding ahead of the horses, lifted both his arms in a widespread gesture as the ground either side grew higher and the valley ahead of him dwindled in width. By rising in the stirrups, Jack was able to communicate with Matt, who was a lot further back on the left flank. Both men knew in advance what they wanted, and nothing untoward happened to complicate their plan. No wildcat intervened as Jack went into the narrows. No low-flying eagle appeared to startle the lead horses.

Matt stayed on the flank as long as possible. Then he swung away, having negotiated the defile and found himself a hiding place behind a smooth rocky outcrop above and on an angle with the exit beyond the defile. Of the horse outfit, young Felipe was the last through. His sharp eyes soon located the spot where Matt had gone to earth, and the latter waved his tobacco-pipe in a farewell gesture as the tail end of the remuda drew away.

* * *

The beeves started to come through within ten minutes. Hatless and prone, Matt was stretched out on a warm flat rock with a good view of the narrow point. He had beside him his water canteen, weapons, a lariat, the spyglass, his stetson and the specially knotted rope to be used at the count.

Backmann, leading the beeves, had an easy job, but he was slow to leave the area of Matt's concealment and the latter wondered if the segundo had any idea about what they were doing. Through came the formidable bell ox, flanked by a few cronies, and then the counting became a chore. Every now and then, a rider came through breaking up the monotonous pattern of stumbling, pushing, butting beeves. Even so soon after the morning start, a half mile separated the first beasts from those at the tail of the herd.

Cloying dust began to cloud the issue at one time, and Matt found his eyes wandering and his counting almost faltering. Small things, like adjusting his hat, or reaching for a drink had him blinking and frowning and recounting two or three animals. A small panic about accuracy stayed with him for a while, and then it passed.

His interest mounted when he realised that the three newcomers were among the last four expected riders to negotiate the gap. Had they detoured? Left their job and the flank exposed? There was a brief dry shout above the noise made by the herd, and then — quite suddenly — all three came together. They were covered in light dust and flapping their hats, and some special interest had put a smile on their habitually hard calculating faces.

A mere handful of steers came through after them. And then it was the turn of the man riding drag. On this occasion, Dan Adler had fallen for the job that no one wanted. He was riding in the dust of all the others. During ordinary work, Adler had a huge fair flowing moustache of the hanging variety, but on this occasion his upper lip appendage was totally hidden by a yellow bandanna which was filtering the air he breathed.

Juan Fuente steered the big chuck wagon through five minutes later. Matt allowed himself to be seen, as he had tired of hiding.

'Why are you, of all people, ridin' back the way we came, Senor Matt?'

'I've been doin' a private count, Juan. At the start, we were three or four over the thousand. Now, we seem to be about eight under. Too many missin' for so few days' travel. Keep it to yourself, will you? I'm supposed to be ahead with Felipe and Jack, you see! *Adios!*'

Juan returned the greeting, waved and went ahead.

★ ★ ★

Walter and Ringo Pierce were brothers. They had started life in the foothills of mountains in the east of Tennessee state, before excessive feuding made it imperative for them to leave home and seek their fortunes further west. In recent years, they had tried their hands at skinning, droving and other everyday western jobs. For six months, they had been seeking to build up a herd of their own without benefit of capital.

Not much progress had been made

that month; not until the infamous trio headed by Link Thompson had shown up once again.

At the time when the herd went through the defile, the two kinsmen were hidden in a small park about one mile east of the drovers' track. Quite near to them, seven or eight beeves were fretting noisily in a pen contrived with ropes linking bushes of mesquite thorn. They were seated on a log. Walter, the lantern-jawed older brother, was shifting a cigar around in his small tight mouth, watching what Ringo, his brother, was drawing on an old creased piece of paper.

'This here big B in a circle is not an easy brand to blotch, Walter. I guess if we had to we could make it look like a Circle S, but I hope we don't have to do anything as drastic as that. What do you think?'

'What do I think?' Walter repeated. Privately, he was thinking that his younger brother ought to shave off his small tuft of chin beard, bright red in colour, but he said: 'I agree with you. It was lucky for us Link an' his partners turned up when they did, but I hope they come soon if they're comin' back at all, 'cause I've heard tell the owner's son is along with the Circle B herd, an' he might be a difficult man to tangle with if he found out what was goin' on. So, let's hope they come soon. We'll give 'em another fifteen minutes. If nothing happens, then we clear out.'

Ringo nodded, and gnawed a lump off a chew of tobacco.

* * *

The bawling of the beeves had warned Matt, and he had approached with sufficient caution to move in unnoticed behind the would-be brand blotchers. Moreover, he had arrived in turn to pick up a few of the brothers' recent exchanges.

If the trio headed by Thompson were coming back again to do business with this pair, then it probably meant more rustled steers were on the way, and possibly an exchange of funds. Enough to catch Backmann's proteges redhanded.

A sudden movement caused by a disturbed snake panicked Matt's sorrel out of its accustomed calm. The Pierces leapt to their feet off the log, but Matt — in their rear — already had a Colt revolver pointed at them.

'Sit yourselves down again, gents, why don't you? Nice an' slow, on account of the heat, eh? If you toss your hardware clear of the log we won't have to make a lot of noise, will we?'

Matt gently massaged one of his prominent ears with the muzzle of his gun before putting it back into an arc between the two men. They were slow to move, but they offered no explanation and they complied.

Walter was allowed to pass a Bull Durham sack across to his brother. They all smoked. Shortly after Ringo's smoke was drawing unevenly, the distant sound of approaching horses was heard.

Link Thompson and Frenchy Dupont, both of whom had fairly shrill voices, came towards the park in a loop, sharing an old joke and laughing hilariously. All three men awaiting them thought they were taking a long time over the last fifty yards, or so.

A muscle in Walter's formidable jaw betrayed what his nerves were doing to him. Ringo's small distinctive beard began to twitch. Matt's teeth closed like a vice on the stem of his tobacco pipe. So tight was his grip on the pipe that when the heavy stone, accurately thrown by the cunning third man, connected with the side of his head, his teeth bit through it.

Burro McNye was the first to reach him. Matt was quickly disarmed and then trussed. Being unconscious he gave his captors no trouble. When he came to, he was the subject of speculation. By straining his neck a little, he could see that the original number of stolen beeves had gone up into double figures. Link Thompson finished counting the notes he had received in payment for the rustled cattle, and then turned his head in the prisoner's direction.

'Too bad we didn't cover his eyes. We could have let him live, if he hadn't seen us.'

Frenchy and Burro both rounded on him. They then stared at each other as if they had not heard properly. The French-Canadian protested.

'Surely, Link. Tell me you ain't gone soft in the head. You wouldn't have spared this galoot to put the word around about us later?'

Thompson laughed heartily. 'Just wanted to be sure you two were listenin', that's all.' He yanked off his weathered hat, stamped on it and eventually punched it into something like its original shape. 'Nope. I was only kiddin'. Of course, he's got to be eliminated. Unless our two buddies, here, have any use for his carcase?'

To the surprise of Ringo, and the other three, Walter Pierce cheerfully took up the offer. 'Sure, leave him to us, amigos, we'll dispose of him for you. When do you think you'll show up again?'

The trio then became cagey. 'Hard to tell in our line of business, Walter. Might be a few weeks, and then again it might be a whole lot sooner. Anyway, we have a good idea where to find you in the future. Why don't you gag that jasper before he starts pleadin'? Me, I can't stand to hear a fellow pleadin' for his life. So unmanly, I always think. Enough to make a man lose his respect for the human race.'

Ringo was the one to apply the gag. Matt glared at him, and protested as he lost the use of his mouth, but it made no difference. After another couple of minutes of small talk, the trio mounted up again and headed due north, aiming to by-pass the defile on the advice of the Pierces.

Matt Hansen squirmed about while

the Pierces strolled unhurriedly, talking and making plans. Any sort of excessive movement seemed to aggravate the unpleasant condition caused by the tight gag. The veteran Texan began to think that his days might well be numbered.

4

After the defile incident the rest of the morning had little to offer by way of diversions. The hours went by until nearly one in the afternoon when Jack consulted Felipe about the terrain they were in and decided where the early camp should be made.

Felipe then rode back to contact Juan on the wagon and make Jack's instructions known. Juan asked his youthful cousin if Matt had shown up again.

'You saw him make his way to the rear, Juan?'

'Sure, he went back, through the defile. He was very thoughtful, as if he was looking for something in particular. I hope no harm has come to him. Maybe he will show up when the meal is served, eh?'

'We shall see, no?' Juan replied, nodding heavily.

* ★ *

Rudy Backmann was a hearty eater. Moreover, he liked to eat as early as possible both at midday and in the evening. This occasion was no exception to his chosen routine. By the time Jack came back to the chuck wagon, most of the other riders were already there, and Rudy was cleaning up the remnants of his substantial meal.

Felipe moved aside to talk to Jack, who shot him an enquiring glance. With his back to the nearest eaters, Felipe repeated what he had learned from his cousin, and made it clear that Matt had not returned. The two parted, and Backmann strolled about, wiping his mouth. Four men had not collected their food, other than Jack. Matt Hansen and the three riders recently signed on.

While Jack was debating what to do, there was a commotion wide of the herd, on the eastern boundary. Out of a cloud of dust came the three riders,

Link, Frenchy and Burro. They were talking loudly, and the gist of what they were saying seemed to suggest that they had recovered two big steers which had gone missing in a mesquite thicket.

Jack wondered about them, but he said nothing. Instead, he switched on a disarming smile. 'Rudy, I want you to do me a favour. I know you've only just finished your meal — '

'Think nothing of it, Jack,' Rudy cut in, beaming in his turn. 'You name it, I'll see to it.'

'I'm grateful, Rudy. I want you to ride ahead. Go beyond the remuda an' chase around until you find Matt Hansen. Due to a misunderstandin' he's still out there some place. It's my fault, too. Send him back, if you find him. I'll send Felipe an' the night guards to join you when we're ready to move. All right?'

'I'll do it. I'll find Matt for you. Consider it done. Have a good meal, and enjoy it. I'll be in touch. *Adios!*'

Backmann made a big play out of

getting on well with the new leader. He shouted a greeting to the three new arrivals, who were dusting themselves down and getting ready to queue up for food. They were still talking rather noisily and appeared to be over-excited.

Jack gave Backmann a couple of minutes to get clear of the camp area, and then he, too, mounted up again and prepared to depart. He whispered to Felipe to tell Juan to keep him some food, and not to make too much fuss about those who were missing.

And then he was off, riding first to westward, and then abruptly southward, in the direction of the defile.

★ ★ ★

For nearly an hour, Jack rode southward on a fresh horse, gradually dropping back towards the defile. He had it in sight quite soon, but as usually happens when a man is in a hurry, the gap seemed to narrow with maddening slowness. He was thirsty and hungry, and yet uppermost in his mind was Matt and Matt's safety. It was fairly obvious that the veteran rider had gone south looking for something. Almost certainly, it had to do with the counting he had been doing as the beeves went through the defile.

Jack was shrewd enough to guess that the numbers had gone down. Probably, Matt had an idea where to look for the missing beasts. He rode through the gap, all his senses alert, his ears reacting to the apparent trapping of sound in the narrowest part. And then he was through the badly trampled area, and coaxing his mount again.

Instinct eventually took him towards the sea of mesquite which had drawn Matt a few hours earlier. A man twanging a mouth harp fuelled his suspicions, and then he was into a small park and almost riding over a writhing trussed body across his path. His mount reared up and practically went out of control, but he checked its waywardness, gave it a short time to cool off and then dismounted.

Matt looked drawn when the gag came off his face. He breathed nosily for a while, and his face was a long time before it relaxed into a grin.

'Mighty glad to see you, amigo. Mighty glad. Thanks, Jack. I'll always be in your debt.'

Jack knelt beside him with the water bottle. 'Who did it, Matt?'

Hansen drank two or three times, miming as he did so the direction of the mouth harpist. He then explained how he had got the drop on the two shifty brothers who had bought Circle B stock. Then, he added how one of the trio had thrown a stone and knocked him out. Eventually, Jack had heard all he wanted to know. He was angry. The time for retribution was at hand.

'If this pair were to kill you, why haven't they done it already? Why haven't they made tracks with their illgotten gains?'

Matt left off massaging his ankles to restore proper circulation. He was beginning to recover his usual good spirits.

'I may sound soft, Jack, but I don't think they were as keen to shoot me as Walter made out. And now, if you ask me, they're sharin' a bottle of whisky, otherwise they'd have been on their way, or reactin' to the sounds of your arrival. The jaspers have my horse somewhere over there, so I'm glad we don't have far to go.'

Suddenly, both men appeared to harden. They checked their hand guns and Jack lovingly ran his hands over his Winchester. 73. 'Okay, Matt, let's go get 'em.'

Anger and an empty stomach made Jack very sharp. On the way in, he had time to think briefly of his girl friend, Dawn. Sun-up to him, in private. And this fellow who had come along to help with the herd on her say-so was her uncle: her mother's brother. A lump rose in his throat as he thought of the girl again. What sort of an impression had he left in her mind, clearing out at such short notice and when she obviously wanted him to stay?

Maybe this trail herd responsibility was forcing him to show a bit of character. Take the weight, for a change, and resist the old craving to take the easy way out.

'You haven't said exactly what you intend to do with these hombres, Jack.'

'That's 'cause I don't know myself. I don't like the jaspers who hang about in these parts an' steal another man's beef. These two are not much different from ordinary rustlers. They ought to be taught a lesson. Let's get a little closer, huh? Then we'll see.'

From a spot within fifty yards, they observed the Pierce brothers through tufts of high grass. Ringo was just about to get another tune out of the mouth harp. Walter removed a cigar from his mouth and used it to conduct the music, which was of poor quality. It was clear from the way they were acting that they had drunk quite a few fingers of whisky.

Jack and Matt exchanged questioning glances, but the initiative lay with Jack. He had the authority, and he carried the only rifle. So, after shrugging his shoulders, he rose slowly to his feet, sighted the Winchester and casually blasted the hat from Walter Pierce's head. The gun shot made a booming clatter. At the same time the mouth harp went silent. Ringo tensed and came to his knees, but his actions were not speedy enough to prevent him sharing his brother's fate. His stetson flew even further, and the two of them were obviously badly shaken as they rose unsteadily to their feet with their hands raised. At first, they were not sure where the shots came from or who was firing them.

'Who's shootin'? If anyone thinks they have grievance against us, why don't you come out into the open an' show yourself? We ain't got anythin' to hide!'

Jack worked the lever of his Winchester very deliberately, and the eyes of the two rogues turned in his direction. He started slowly towards them, his senses alert and the weapon in a handy position.

'How can you say that to Jack Brogan, owner of the Circle B herd? Are you about to pretend you didn't steal or purchase my beef before I got here?'

Walter Pierce blinked. His brother looked visibly shaken.

'Who says we stole your beef, mister?' Ringo enquired.

He was playing for time. Nothing much could be gained in an argument along those lines. By way of an answer, Matt Hansen rose into view and sauntered off in the direction of his missing horse. While Jack rounded up the Pierces' weapons and secured their wrists behind them Matt collected his mount and walked it back to the scene of the temporary camp. He then moved away again, located the stolen cattle and came back to report.

'Ten head, all bearin' the Circle B

markings, Mr Brogan.' Suddenly he turned on his former persecutors. 'How much did you pay Thompson for them?'

Walter filled his lungs, and appeared to be on the verge of an argument, but Jack brought up the muzzle of his Winchester.

'Don't say you didn't pay, otherwise you take what's comin' to you! Where I come from, we hang rustlers. Today, a bullet would be speedier. How much?'

'Ten bucks a head, mister. Times is hard, an' a couple of small time operators like my brother an' me don't have much of a chance to build a herd without cuttin' a few corners. Most of the big herds further south belong to fellows who borrowed a few head to get started. Ain't that so?'

Jack was beginning to think Walter was getting too sure of himself, once again. He gave him a sharp talking to for hinting that his father was once a rustler and turned the two unfortunates over to Matt, while he himself retired from the action and helped himself to what was left of the Pierces' stew.

Matt, for his part, told a painful story about what Thompson and his buddies were likely to do to the two Pierces when they learned what had happened. He then took away their boots, tied all their weapons, as well as the boots, to their saddles and sent them off towards the east, on foot.

If the riding horses knew their way, and the Pierces did not do anything foolish, they would be shod again and back in the saddle inside thirty minutes.

★ ★ ★

It was nearly four-thirty in the afternoon when Dan Adler, riding drag for the day, first looked around and saw the small cloud of dust catching up with him. Another fifteen minutes was time enough for the eleven recovered beeves to be restored to the main herd.

The drag man removed his dust mask long enough to talk to Jack and Matt, and to confirm that the number of beasts they had with them was eleven.

After drinking water, the two dusty riders then gradually moved up the side of the herd. They passed the man riding swing, another wide on the left flank, and then they sighted Rudy Backmann returning from his unfruitful search ahead of the herd for Matt Hansen.

Rudy looked to be in a very bad mood at first glance, but when he saw the other two his visage changed perceptibly. Backmann gave his mount a touch of the rowel.

'So you found him! Well that's great! But how come he turned up at the rear of the herd instead of out front?'

'You sure you don't already know, Rudy?' Jack asked calmly.

'Sure I'm sure I don't know. What are you gettin' at? I didn't send him any place, did I?'

'Maybe not,' Jack agreed, after a short pause. 'This mornin' Matt counted up the total number of the herd. As soon as he had finished, he decided that we were losin' animals too quickly. So he turned around, went back through the defile an' discovered a small park where about seven head were located. The jaspers who had bought them were there, too. Matt got the drop on them, but a little later he had a spot of misfortune. The cunnin' rascals who sold Circle B cattle turned up again with some more. If they'd had their way, Matt would be dead by now. Your friends sure are pretty deadly, ain't they, Rudy?'

'Hey, wait a minute, will you? I'm just a simple cowpuncher. Will you spell out your accusations? Say who you are accusin'?'

Matt cleared his throat. 'I think you already know, but anyway, we're talkin' of Link Thompson, Frenchy Dupont an' Burro McNye. Yer, quite familiar names, men introduced by you, personally.'

'How can you be sure all this is true?' Backmann had paled, in spite of his tan.

'I rescued Matt. The testimony of the Pierce brothers. Matt's own testimony. If I waited till all the crew were together, say at night camp, an' then told them about three rustlers among their number, your buddies would be shot to doll rags, Rudy.' Jack pointed an accusing finger, and raised his voice. 'They've worked this rustlin' caper many times before, an' salivated any man who happened to get in their way! If they had killed Matt, if I hadn't found him in time, I'd have ordered the crew to wipe out your rustlin' buddies, an' you, too, Rudy, an' don't you forget it!'

The muscles in the segundo's jaw worked this way and that, his eyes glinted so that he had to look away. It was over a minute before he could trust himself to speak coherently.

'All right, I'm sorry. So, what do you want me to do?'

'I'm glad you asked that, Rudy. From here on in, Matt an' me, we're goin' to part company for a while. Between the two of us, we're goin' to inform all honest members of the crew to be on the lookout for rustlers, especially the ones you brought along. And they are to shoot on sight, if Thompson and his buddies show up again. Three crew members already know what's happenin' so the rest won't take long.

'As for you, you have to deliver the message to them to quit. No notice, only a warnin'. No pay to come. Thompson took one hundred and ten dollars from the buyers. You have to get that dinero from him, an' be ready to hand it to me the next time we meet.

'Tell your buddies to turn in the brand horses they're usin' an' collect the three crowbait horses they arrived on. After that, they ride westward. Immediately, an' without contactin' anyone. Any deviation from these instructions an' you part company with us, too. If you happen to go with them, we'll stop the herd an' start man huntin'. Okay, Rudy? Well that's it. Adios.'

The segundo hesitated for a few seconds, and then he started across the herd, a very tricky thing to do in ordinary circumstances. However, he used his experience with beeves and refrained from causing a stampede or a mill.

'There's he goes,' Matt remarked gently. 'If he's innocent of this, I reckon we'll still have trouble with him later.'

'My sentiments also, Matt. You come along with me as far as point. Me, I'll ride on an' ramrod the remuda again. Be on the alert in case the trio try anything tricky.'

As they gradually approached the leading beeves, Matt said: 'Jack, I came along with this outfit because Dawn felt you might not be able to cope. You're ramroddin' the whole shebang like a veteran. I don't figure I was necessary, honestly.'

Jack grinned and really felt good. 'Thanks for sayin' so, Matt, an' for comin' along. You think Dawn will still be keen on me, when I get back?'

'You know the answer to that without me tellin' you. Of course she'll be keen. Absence makes the heart grow fonder. Didn't you ever hear that, Jack?'

Presently, they parted on excellent terms. Before six in the evening the trio of renegades made a brief visit to the remuda, collected their own horses and lit out for the west.

Just in earshot, Link Thompson slowed his horse and waved his rifle. 'You cow nurses ain't heard the last of us yet!'

'We'll be in touch!' McNye promised, in his shrill voice.

One rifle shot, fired by Matt Hansen, flew very close over Thompson's head before the trio resumed, and went on out of sight. Backmann returned the rustled cow money, in full, without comment, prior to supper.

5

For three days after the departure of the unwanted trio, the Circle B droving outfit hit a series of minor drawbacks, none of which had to do with the men.

On one occasion, the all-important chuck wagon lost a wheel and several hours were needed in which to effect a repair sufficiently durable to counter the extremely taxing conditions of the trail. Nowhere was the going easy. Nowhere were there tracks intended for coaches, buckboards or wagons. The underhangings of all wheeled vehicles had to take a hammering which stressed the planks and timbers, and sometimes resulted in a bent axle.

When the wagon was out of action, the crew suffered privations and their morale, as a direct result, suffered.

Within a day of the wagon's being

repaired, serious difficulties occurred with the natural water supply. Towards the northern limits of the Edwards Plateau, small scattered lakes — sometimes referred to by cattlemen as the Indian Lakes — failed as a regular supply. There were upwards of a dozen of these small reservoirs of water, so useful to anyone taking a herd over a long distance. On this particular trip, it was discovered at the last minute that the three or four southernmost lakes had dried out. In order to water the cattle at eventide, it was necessary to protract the day's work by almost two hours. That meant extra long spells in the saddle, and hundreds of red-eyed beeves developing a fractious mood. This mood spread from the least fit to the fittest and gave the night guards a few shocks, even when water had been discovered and most of the beasts satisfied.

★　★　★

Pineville was a small western town which had its origins through mining, ranching and farming. It was situated perhaps five miles west of the main route used by drovers from southern Texas heading north. Jack Brogan had it on his itinerary as a possible calling place, in the event of a serious deficiency in supplies, funds or horses.

However, Jack had not even thought about towns in the hectic few days which had engulfed him and his crew since the incident with the rustlers and the brand blotchers. In fact, the hard-worked outfit would have bypassed the town without giving it any consideration, had it not been for a stranger arriving from Pineville, right out of the blue — totally unexpected — on the ninth day of travel.

At ten in the morning, Jack was scouting ahead of the herd and the remuda, depressingly punishing himself with thoughts about it having been his fault over the water shortage. He should have thought to ride north, or send someone in his stead, to make sure that there was water in the southern Indian Lakes, even if the said lakes had been there for maybe a century or more.

A man with a herd of long-legged longhorned southern beeves just did not take chances about supplies enroute.

Jack had shaved twice since he set off, and yet he had permanent reddish-brown stubble on his chin and a set of crowsfeet wrinkles at the outer ends of his eyes which made him seem a good deal more mature than he had been when he left home.

He thought aloud. 'Only a quarter of the way there, an' Texas seems a million miles away. And that's a fool thought, because the earth under our feet is still Texas. A long way from San Antone, nevertheless. I wonder if there are any more setbacks ahead of us to take their toll of me before we hit Kansas?'

Having said so much, he became quietly pensive again. He was further ahead of the main bunch than he had intended to be. Possibly, his conscience about earlier oversights had pushed him forward. And he had been lucky, this far . . .

Two kinds of sound began to impinge upon his ears. One was the distant sound of moving water, subdued by distance to a low roar, and the other was a much more fleeting, ephemeral kind of sound. Music. The sort of music so often conjured up in the west with a small instrument. Mouth organ music. Somehow, the two types of music seemed to fade into one another at times. He stopped feeling that he was imagining one of them as the other grew more pronounced.

He knew that somewhere ahead of him there was an east-west watercourse. Moving water. Either a minor tributary of the Colorado River, or something of a similar nature which ran into the Brazos. It was of no consequence which turbulent river accepted this lesser one. The only matter of any serious consequence was how to get a herd across it without unnecessary difficulties.

Distantly, the mouth organ floated to him a few bars of 'Dixie'. At the same time, Jack was amused and suspicious. Who would want to announce his presence ahead of a trail herd by offering music while the crew was working. Furthermore, this far, he had only found renegades along the line of travel. Nevertheless, the coming encounter made a break with monotony and could quite well prove interesting.

Fifteen minutes later, a strapping bay horse — chosen because of its seemingly unlimited stamina — carried the dry youthful trail boss up the slight gradient which ended in the banks of the stream.

Jack reined in at the top of the slope, crooked one leg round his saddle horn, and dropped his shoulders in resignation.

He beheld thirty, possibly forty yards of creaming vital water. On either bank, a small cliff of ten to twelve feet and in the centre a deep colour which hinted at unplumbable depths.

He yawned heartily without thinking about covering his mouth. At the same time, the mouth organ which he had heard earlier, struck up a military marching tune which suggested the civil war of a few years back.

'Are you thinkin' of givin' that horse a swim, or would you prefer it just to paddle?'

The voice making the enquiry was high-pitched, seemingly educated and well modulated.

Jack turned his attention sharply in the direction of the enquiry. As the organ music had cut out just before the question, obviously the questioner was also the musician. A gaudily painted travelling salesman's wagon, parked on the north side of the water in a slight hollow, flanked by screening trees, provided a backcloth to the other human, who was sitting up and forward in a battered wooden chair capable of several useful positions.

Lounging and cropping in the background, half a dozen well fed mules worked on the short grass nurtured by creek water.

'Good day to you, sir,' Jack remarked politely. 'In answer to your question, I don't have to make the crossin' at all until later in the day. However, on second thoughts, I believe I will cross over and join you, just for the experience. Unless you wouldn't advise it at this spot?'

The lounging man made a play with his mobile brows, sending them up and down on his forehead. His crown was quite devoid of hair. Dark shadows on his creased face showed where he had shaved with a sharp cut-throat razor that very morning. A grey cutaway coat hung on the back of the all-purpose chair. The hand which did not hold the edible meat hovered round the arm hole of a gaudy waistcoat coloured like the stars and stripes of the American flag.

The stranger burped. 'If you want to

make it to this bank in time to sample the remnants of this wine, you'd better start upstream a couple of lariat's length, at least.'

A wine bottle, one third full, was on the grass beside the chair along with a dove-grey beaver skin hat. As Jack turned his mount, intending to take the proffered advice, the stranger called after him.

'By the way, my name is Solomon C. Jones. I'm a businessman. Don't forget to slacken your saddle, eh?'

'Be with you in a couple of minutes,' Jack promised. Solomon C. Jones was a successful con-man and general grafter.

At one time he had joined up in the army of the Union, but being unhappy about constant manoeuvres and taking orders from others, he had slipped away from a battle field where the battle was little more than a skirmish of half-tried troops, and since then he had been on the move.

While the war dragged on, he moved around in his first vehicle, stealing and selling and keeping out of harm's way by affecting a limp which — so he said — had kept him out of the armed forces. In fact, the limp was created by wearing a boot with a pebble in it while in company.

Apart from the stealing of property, he also purloined information. It was an easy matter to give intelligence to the forces of one side about troop movements connected with the other. As a spy, he made quite a useful income. In time, he was on the secret payroll of a brigadier on one side and a full colonel on the other.

When the war was over he did some carpet-bagging, but his dislike for ordinary everyday transport sent him back to his first love, that of trading from his own vehicle.

He had broken the law on many an occasion, but no one had ever put him away for longer than a day in a cell.

Pineville was a useful temporary headquarters for such a merchant, especially as he wanted his reputation to cool down in counties further west and east. When business flagged in town, he came out on one of these forays to intercept a trail crew on its way north. His meeting with Jack Brogan was timely. He had offered his services ten or eleven times on previous occasions, but this spring he had not — this far — done any out-of-town business. Moreover, he was bored.

He rose from his chair quite smoothly being rather more muscular than his stocky frame at first suggested. After filling up a clean wine glass out of his bottle, he set it down firmly on the ground and strolled over to the water's edge to watch the newcomer's progress.

Jack Brogan was as adept in water as he was on land. Fortunately, this mount — a willing bay — liked exercise in water as much as he did. It swam strongly with its neck extended out in front and its nostrils dilated. Half way across, the sudden increase of strength in the current gave it a few bad moments. At that point, Solly Jones dug his heels into the bank and prepared to witness the young Texan's discomfiture. Brogan, however, slipped out of the saddle, swam alongside the struggling horse and avoided its hind legs until he had a good purchase on its tail. In that position, horse and man completed the crossing, and the man qualified for the glass of red wine which awaited him.

'Congratulations, young man, you tackled that slight hazard very well for one of your age. I'm a little bit out of condition, myself, and I wouldn't have liked to take the swim on a full stomach. How do you like the wine?'

Side by side, the wet and dry humans strolled back to the spot where the colourful wagon rested.

'Tastes good, an' has a nice bouquet, too. French, I'd say. You didn't import it yourself, did you?'

Jones chuckled. 'No, as a matter of fact I bought several dozen bottles from the cellar of a big old house where the owner was down on his luck. Tell me, are you a loner, or do you work for a trail herd boss?'

Jack squatted easily beside the chair and casually dried himself with a towel which Jones had supplied. It had a pile on it like expensive carpet.

'I'm Jack Brogan, of the Circle B ranch in San Antone. Our family sends beef north all the time. This is my first trip, however, and I'm doin' a spot of scoutin'. Seekin' an easy way across this waterway. One where the herd won't get frightened, won't get out of hand or get drowned. How well do you know the river, Mr Jones?'

Jones massaged himself around the waistcoat, as though aiding his digestion. His sinewy hands encountered a box of small cigars, which he brought out with due care. Stripped to the waist, Jack took one and expressed his thanks. It occurred to him that Jones was the first 'outsider' other than the rustlers and blotchers whom he had met since he left home.

Talking through fragrant smoke, Jones

replied: 'Oh, I know this stretch of the creek, Sunset Creek, that is, like the back of my hand, Jack. Now, if you want to save yourself some time and a whole lot of bother, I could help you. You help me, an' I'll help you. What do you say?'

By this time, Jack was strolling around fully stripped off, with the towel wrapped around his waist.

'In the event that I agree, how can I help you?'

Jones beamed, disarmingly. 'I'm a salesman. I sell things, an' I give a service. Say I was to roll along beside or near your outfit for a day or two. Your boys are a long way from town, from the amenities, as you might say. I can sell them almost anything, everything that a smart young herdsman might want to freshen himself up. And provide a little useful diversion into the bargain. My visits are popular with other trail herds, Jack. They could be with yours.'

'What sort of diversions, Solomon?'

'Solly rests more easily on the lips. Apart from ordinary sellin' I can provide facilities for a bit of social gamblin'. Roulette, whist, pontoon, you name it. I can tell fortunes, too, if anyone needs that sort of service. What do you say?'

Jack came to a standstill with his cigar cocked at an impressive angle. 'This here is a *gamblin*' rig? Is that what you're sayin' Solly?'

Solly beamed some more. He produced a soiled card deck from the pocket of his grey cutaway coat and did two or three sleight of hand tricks with the cards. Having produced all the aces from inside his grey beaver hat, he continued with the picture cards, in descending order of merit, until Jack began to look impatient.

'Sure, that's the Solly Jones gamblin' rig, for all to see, and to inspect, if anyone thinks they can't trust the owner. Go take a look, why don't you?'

Jack nodded and took up the offer, and while he was doing so, Jones strolled with him. 'For your information, Jack, the ford you seek is about three-quarters of a mile upstream. I'm gamblin' you'll use that valuable piece of information, an' that I'll be allowed to do some tradin' with your boys.'

Jones' ingratiating manner, along with his obvious facilities in card manipulating intrigued Jack, who loved gambling himself.

'Tell you what I'll do, Solly. I'll ride down to the ford on this side an' cross by it. If it's as good as you say, we'll use it, later in the day an' you'll be welcome at our night camp. How will that be?'

Jones juggled with his grey topper. 'That sure as hell sounds fine to me, amigo. I'll be at the crossing this side, when you and your beeves arrive, an' I'll take you up on your offer for tonight. Have another cigar, an' look forward to a pleasant evenin'.'

Jack left shortly afterwards, his thirst slaked, his mind full of pleasant distractions and with confidence about the coming crossing. All he felt uncertain of was whether he should himself indulge in a spot of gambling.

6

The ford crossing at the spot designated by Solly Jones was immaculate. No beeves were lost, and few animals became jittery through over-excitement which usually affected them at a water crossing. On the north side, Jones vamped tune after tune on his mouth organ, using so much volume in his work that all the trail crew knew of his presence before half the steers were across.

The midday halt was a little later than usual, but no one cared on account of the herd having been watered and the water obstacle being behind them. The rest of the day could be anticipated as one with no hazards.

In a huge kite-shaped area bordered by two narrow converging streams, shallow in depth, Jack organised the settling down of the herd for the night.

All the crew were in a perky mood. Jones was anxious to get started with his business. To slow him down a bit, they invited him to take his food from the chuck wagon. Further, Jack insisted that the gambling rig should be secured across the shallows on the west side, to minimise distracting noises which might affect the herd after bedding down.

Jones' went a bit harder when he heard of the restrictions, but he agreed and also said that he would cut out the music during the evening session. Soon, the meal was over. The duty night guards looked glum, but Jones promised faithfully to keep his premises open until such time that any man, whatever his duty, could get along there and buy things, or take a hand at cards.

As things got under way, Jack took a stroll with Matt.

'He's a distraction, all right,' the older man agreed, 'but will he be good for morale, ultimately, or bad? You can never be sure that hombres who come out from town are basically honest. Me, I wouldn't have him around too long.'

'I promised him this evenin' Matt. So I can't do anything about what's happenin' now.'

They paused in their strolling. By straining the ears a little it was possible to detect the clattering roll of the ball as it bounced round the roulette wheel, on its way to the winning number.

'A block of soap, a hair brush an' that sort of thing. They're not bad for morale,' Matt murmured. 'We all like to gamble, but is gamblin' good for us all? It's the money angle which is difficult. Felipe said he's already offered to loan money to one or two of the hands. They don't have much. What do you think? Is it good they're in debt to him?'

Jack shook his head very decidedly. 'I don't like that side of the business, at all. Tell you what I'll do. I'll offer every man a loan. Twenty dollars, an' no more. After that, I'm not settlin' any man's debts, however much the amount happens to be. Somebody ought to go over there an' tell 'em.'

At that point, Rudy Backmann materialised. From a roll in his money belt, Jack produced some two hundred dollars. 'Rudy, offer each man twenty against his pay. No one is to run into debt with this hombre, or to make any sort of promises to him. Can I ask if you've ever met him before?'

The segundo, who was still smarting inwardly over the business of the three rustlers and his own loss of face, nevertheless, shook his head very decidedly. 'Solomon Jones is entirely new to me. Thanks for trustin' me with the funds. I'll mosey over there, right now.'

After the segundo had gone, the other two were in a thoughtful mood.

Jack said: 'Either Rudy is in a contrite mood, or he's a better actor than we ever thought he was. Still, I fear we have to be vigilant as far as he's concerned. Now, I'm thinkin' of takin' a turn as night guard to prevent any bad feelin' among the lads on night duty.'

Matt at once agreed to do the same. Jack beamed and promised him a bonus when the time came. They went about saddling and taking over in a fine humour.

* * *

Day break and the need for early morning coffee brought away the last of the late night roisterers from the vicinity of the gambling rig.

Jack had only catnapped during the night, and he was on hand to chat with the last two gamblers as they strolled back to the camp site with their hands thrust deep into their empty pockets and glum expressions on their tired faces.

Of the two hundred dollars doled out to the hands, Solomon Jones had acquired all except thirty. None of them grumbled. They had gambled and lost. At no time did anyone think that he was being cheated. The odds were against the gambler, and the men had lost. Jones, cunning businessman as he was, made sure that every loser had a gift of some sort. Combs, pipes, tobacco sacks were among the offerings. The gifts helped to keep the men sweet, and yet Jack Brogan felt that one night of gambling was enough.

That day, he kept the men and the herd moving at a goodly rate. By the end of midday camp, all the hands knew that the Boss had no intention of lending out any more money for gambling. Furthermore, Brogan expected Jones to take his leave before evening camp.

In order to make sure that Jones broke off his association with the Circle B drovers, Jack intimated to the travelling man that he intended to visit the nearby town himself, and that he would appreciate Jones going along with him as a guide.

Solomon, aware that no more money was going to circulate among the riders, settled for the guide's job, and took Jack aboard his rig for the trip into town. All the time they were riding,

Jones talked about gambling incidents in his life, and the way Jack enthused over the stories made him think that the trail boss himself could be separated from some of his funding money.

* * *

Clearly, Solly Jones knew a lot of people in Pineville. Also, he had a way of ingratiating himself with people old and new. Jack had enjoyed riding on the box of the wagon, and he showed only polite surprise when Jones pulled up outside the livery at the east end of town and gave orders for Jack's led horse, the chestnut, to be taken indoors and groomed and fed. Jones really surprised him by paying in advance for the liveryman's services.

Jack protested. 'Ain't no need for you to pay my dues, Solly. I've got the means of funds, an' I'd prefer to pay myself.'

Jones lifted his grey beaver hat, guffawed in loud amusement, and set the hat back on his bald forehead. 'Don't be so sensitive, Jack. I'm only returnin' a favour. Besides, you might run out of ready funds, if you avail yourself of the gamblin' opportunities in this fair town. Let me advise you. Take a bath. Get yourself a few spare sets of clothes, right? Take in a meal, if you're hungry. Then, an' only then, think about relaxin' a bit yourself. I guess you'd have been over to my rig last evenin' if you hadn't got the responsibility for the crew an' the herd. Now, ain't I right?'

Some of the fancy mode of talk had left the travelling man's speech as he talked now. As they progressed between two sets of false fronts, viewing peeling boards, shady sidewalks, advertisements for this and that, Matt found himself smiling. The evening was still young. A lot could happen before he needed to be back with the herd around dawn.

'All right, Solly, I'll take a bath, haircut and shave, buy me some new levis an' shirts, have a meal then go out on the town. Now, where do I get me a bath?'

Jones bellowed with laughter. He parked his rig, took Jack into a hotel for a drink, and then turned him over to the proprietor to arrange for the bath and advise about other things.

★ ★ ★

By half past eight, Jack had made all his preparations. He sauntered out of the hotel wearing a new blue shirt, a matching bandanna, new levis and a neat cream-coloured side-rolled stetson. His chin and face were cleared of hair, his sideburns and crown had seen the shears and for once he looked like the prosperous owner of a Texas trail herd. Solomon Jones was waiting for him at the first table inside the batwing doors of the Lone Pine saloon. Jones was half way through a big cigar, and wearing a new grey beaver hat with two small tinted feathers stuck in the band.

'Ah, there you are, Jack! Come on

over here, make yourself at home. The Lone Pine is used to cattlemen on the move. Take a shot out of my whisky bottle. Sometimes I supply the saloon, other times they supply me. Always the best brew.'

Jack soon entered into the spirit of the smoke-laden building. He sank down into an upright chair and let his eyes rove around the assembled men at leisure. The establishment had two bars. One long one, in the back of the building, and a shorter one behind the baize tables occupied by regular evening gamblers.

The two of them talked of horses, travel, interesting acquaintances and different notions of how to spend a leisure evening. Inevitably, Jack's interest turned to the roulette wheel, with its horseshoe crowd of gamblers and watchers. Jones' glinting eyes also mirrored a great interest in the wheel, which was much bigger than the one he carried around in his rig.

After sinking a few fingers of whisky,

they sauntered over and placed some wagers on the squares. Jones won the second time. Jack kept doubling from his starter of one dollar, so that in a little over forty minutes, he had run through the balance of all the folded notes he had with him, notes still in hand after advancing the men twenty apiece for their gambling in the Jones rig.

The excitement of gambling, losing and drinking fairly steadily soon had Jack keyed up. He wanted to do well in front of this casual acquaintance, this commerical gambler, but his money was done almost before he was launched.

Jones topped up his glass as he backed away from the chairs used by the principal gamblers.

'Are you bothered about your losses, Jack?' Jones wanted to know. 'I'd have said you were a poker player, but if you want to cut your losses an' get back to the herd, why, I won't stop you. All I had in mind was to see you enjoyed a short spell away from responsibility.'

Jack breathed out cigar smoke. 'My losses don't bother me, Sol. Not at all. I'm entitled to squander a few dollars out of the funds set up to mount this herdin' operation. The thing is, I can't get me any funds this late at night, even though I have a bill signed by my father, Clinton Brogan, so I don't see that I have an alternative.'

Jones laughed. 'If that's all that's botherin' you, amigo, *I* can finance you, in a manner of speakin'. Why don't I advance you a hundred dollars out of my own pocket? You can give me an IOU for the bank in the mornin'. You can't see him now, but the local banker is in the buildin' right now. He plays a few hands at poker, himself. He's called Jasper Bates. Playin' partners, Henry Levine, the lawyer, an' Ossie Trendall, the undertaker. I usually make up the four myself when I'm in town, but if you want to take my place, you're surely welcome. What do you say?'

'You're a very accommodatin' friend,

Sol,' Jack remarked gushingly. The liquor was beginning to affect him. 'If you are sure you don't mind, then I will take your place with the bank manager an' those other two you mentioned. Where do they operate?'

'In a private room, off the balcony, Jack. I'll take you up there right away, if you want to make an immediate start. Let's go.'

Before they went into the upper room, Jones handed over one hundred dollars in notes. 'I'll introduce you, have you sign your bill, an' then I'll leave you. If you want anythin' further, I'll be down below. Don't hesitate to call on me again. Here, have another cigar. You'll enjoy that. The boys in there will see to your drinks.'

Jones knocked. A voice said: 'If that's you, Jonesy, come on in!'

The travelling man chuckled. He opened the door, ushered Jack in in front of him, and began the introductions. There was a desk with a scarred and stained top against one wall, and a South American macaw in a large metal cage on a chest at the other side.

'Gents, this is Jack Brogan, of the Circle B ranch in San Antonio. This is his only night in town, so I hoped you wouldn't mind if he sat in on your game. He has funds. I've just seen to that. All I'm stickin' around for is his note, which I intend to bring to the bank in the mornin'.'

They all made cordial noises, and Jack began to feel welcome at the outset.

Jasper Bates, the banker, was a well-groomed man of fifty stripped to a grey waistcoat, and with his spectacles up on his forehead. Levine, the lawyer, was sitting well back to avoid the smoke from Bates' pipe. Levine had thin brows and a seamy complexion. The green eyeshade accentuated his receding hair. Ossie Trendall, the undertaker, was the oldest of the trio. He had white hair and buck teeth, and when he was not manipulating cards he toyed with a home-rolled cigarette.

Jack backed away and seated himself at the desk. He frowned over the actual wording of the IOU until Jones discovered a model from which to copy in the desk drawer.

For a few moments, the parrot snorted, the paste-boards moved crisply, and the banker whistled under his breath. Jack was writing.

To the Manager,
The Pineville Cattlemen's Association Bank.
Please pay to Solomon Jones from the funds arrangement of Mr Clinton Brogan of the Circle B ranch, San Antonio, Texas, the sum of $100, and oblige.

Jack Brogan.
(signed)

Jones received the paper with a benign smile. 'Perhaps you could just show Jasper, there, your father's letter of authorisation, Jack?'

The young Texan hastened to comply. Bates glanced at the letter briefly, then looked keenly into Jack's face, and nodded.

'Sure, sure, young fellow. I've seen that writing before. Your Pa has a fine style of handwriting, I'll be bound. Put the letter away, an' make sure you don't lose it.'

Jack then took his place, and the play began. Jones slipped out without being missed. At first, all three town residents appeared to take life easy. The banker offered his tobacco pouch. The undertaker held out the makings, but Jack settled for one of lawyer Levine's cigars, having forgotten that he had a spare one in his pocket. Smoke whirled slowly around under the shade above the table. A barman brought in fresh glasses and a second bottle of spirits.

Jack's luck was mixed. His calling was good and not so good. He played in a pleasant alcoholic haze, chuckled when money came his way, and made light of his ill fortune when he lost.

When he shuffled the cards and did the cutting, he was amusing, dextrous even, but it was clear within the first hour that he was not about to amass a fortune at the expense of the regular players. In fact, he was going to lose.

The hand which was going to reduce his funds to two or three dollars began in the run up to midnight. The play became slower. No one seemed to mind. Eventually, the banker consulted his watch, announced that the witching hour was at hand, and asked if anyone was ready to retire.

Jack made an openhanded gesture, yawned and burped, and excused himself.

'If it's all the same to you gents, I'll take this opportunity to leave the action. Jones, Jonesy is still on the premises, an' as he said earlier, I'm due back with my outfit before sun-up. So, if no one objects . . . '

No one did, and a short while later, he found himself leaving the saloon with his arm across Jones' shoulders.

Jack had not been quite himself since he mentioned sun-up. For a time, he did not know what it was that bothered him. Then it came back to him. 'Sun-up.' His own personal and private nickname for his girl, back in San Antone. He began to feel a deep longing for her, and inwardly he was asking himself why in the world he was where he was, hundreds of miles away from home, ramrodding a thousand head of steers, instead of enjoying life around the Circle B and whooping it up with his girl.

He had a few moments of clarity when Jones boosted him into the saddle of his horse, checked that he had all his belongings with him, and pointed out the direction he had to take.

Nothing happened to mar his ride back to the night camp. His mind was full of maudlin sentimental thoughts about home and his girl. In the back of his mind was the notion that Solomon C. Jones was one of nature's western gentlemen.

He would not have been so contented if he had known that Jones intended to 'doctor' the IOU before he presented it. Jones aimed to receive one thousand dollars, instead of one hundred. All he had to do was add a nought to Jack's figures, and ten times the money loaned would be handed over to the travelling man.

7

In some ways, the events round about Jones' visit, and the trip into town marked a turning point for Jack Brogan in regard to his ability as a trail boss, and in his relationship with the regular drovers.

Before Pineville, Jack had worked hard, but he had been inclined to involve himself solely with the remuda and with only two or three of the hands. After that period, he made his own routine more flexible, mixing more with the herd and the men whose primary duties were based on the herd, rather than on the horses. Backmann and Hansen were among the first to notice the change in their leader, and gradually the others came round to the same point of view.

Matt Hansen was pleased. He mulled over what he was learning, and kept his own thoughts strictly to himself. Backmann acted similarly, except that — on occasion — he passed remarks about Brogan never having been properly tested. A proper emergency was all that was needed to separate the men from the boys. The days slipped by. Backmann waited.

The Texas town of Abilene became a subject of speculation on the men's lips, but no one came out to make contact with them and a conference between Jack, Juan and Rudy confirmed that there was no commodity that they were desperately short of. And so Abilene had little effect upon them and the progress they were making.

Backmann still had cronies. In fact, in secret he had made a bet with Adler, Rossi and Butch Malone that the Thompson trio would show up again and make trouble. As the days slipped by, first one and then another of these three would saunter up to the segundo and ask him when he was prepared to pay out, because Thompson, Dupont and McNye had not shown up and the distance between the herd and the trio's happy hunting ground was getting greater all the time.

Some ten days after Pineville, Backmann promised to honour his bets within thirty days of the herd having left San Antone. If he was not pestered to death with niggling enquiries in the meantime. None of the trio who had made bets with him had any doubts about him. He did not want to pay out, and he was hoping that they would forget all about the two dollars each which he owed them long before thirty days was up. So, Dan Adler, Pete Rossi and Malone left the segundo alone, but they never ceased to remind one another of the passage of time.

As Butch said: 'A fellow who has said a number, like thirty days, can't really go back on his promise, so long as we all keep him up to it. Ain't that right?'

Pete and Dan agreed. They had patience. They could wait. In the intervening days, there was nothing in particular that they could spend two dollars on, and so the delay did not really matter.

As they travelled north, the spring sunshine brought on the new grass. The big rivers, with their many tributaries, provided an ample and ready supply of water for the animals, even if slight hazards came with them. A couple of days saw them beyond the Brazos. Three days were sufficient to negotiate the tributaries of the mighty Red River which for miles formed the boundary line between Texas and Oklahoma territory. Crossing a river or a creek became almost a daily occurrence. Each rider had a favourite swimming horse and he kept to it, deliberately saving his swimmer for the special occasions.

On the twenty-ninth day, Adler, Rossi and Malone got together at the midday halt and had a small argument about the progress of the calendar. They were not absolutely sure whether that day was, in fact, the twenty-ninth or the thirtieth.

However, Backmann had been in a bad temper for nearly two days, and as he was difficult to get along with, they declined to question him about the number of the days. They were wise, in that respect.

A new problem, one which this crew had not experienced before, had cropped up early that morning. Since dawn, a strong breeze had blown from the east. The wind, in itself, did them no harm: nor did it complicate their labours. It simply meant that the dust all went in one direction and, in a way, the work of the men who controlled the left flank and 'swing' of the herd, became less desirable than that of the person riding 'drag' at the rear.

The dust was something all the riders were used to. The warmth of the breeze and the easily discernible smell of wood smoke was new, and disturbing. It meant that the beeves became nervous. Instinctively, wood smoke told them of a timber fire. Although the conflagration was some little distance away, the instincts of the animals promoted fear.

Being fearful, the beasts were that much more difficult to control and pressure was put upon the drovers. Ahead of the four-footed outfit was yet another great waterway. The Canadian meandered across the Panhandle, the last of the great rivers of Texas, but this next one, the Cimarron, was partly in the Oklahoma territory strip and partly in the state of Kansas.

Their destination was only a few more days away, and Jack had somehow dredged up some more enthusiasm for the job in hand. At two in the afternoon, he took off on his favourite horse to get ahead of the herd. He had Felipe Fuente with him, mounted on a rangy dun gelding, and they made it to the waters of the Cimarron inside two hours.

'Ain't no signs of a ford hereabouts, Felipe,' Jack pointed out. 'Like I was sayin' back at midday camp, all that smoke has swung the herd off the regular track. We're two or maybe three miles west of the ford drovers normally use.'

Felipe also was feeling the heat, due to the riding effort. He pushed his hat down the back of his neck and mopped himself in a workman-like fashion. 'Sure, sure, Senor Jack. We're too far west, but it doesn't mean we're in a hopeless position. There must be other crossings used by trail herds. We can soon figure out the position. What do you say? Do we separate?'

Jack frowned, reacting rather wearily. 'I guess so, Felipe. The obvious alternative would be to work the whole herd east along this bank. It could be done, even with the water drawin' the beeves, but with that darned wood smoke blowin' right in their faces, we'd be askin' for real trouble. What do you say we meet back here in one hour?'

The young Mexican agreed, and turned off to westward. Jack went off in the other direction. For perhaps fifteen minutes, young Brogan pushed his chestnut to a good speed, but after that he lost confidence in what he was doing. The river looked anything but fordable. There was a ferry, of sorts, further east, but no ferryman would use his conveyance for cattle in large numbers . . .

So Jack turned back, soon reached the point where he had left his partner, and then he followed up Felipe's route because a kind of desperation was driving him. Felipe had covered more ground than he had expected. Jack caught his first glimpse of Fuente when the Mexican came out of bankside scrub some three hundred yards away. They waved, acknowledging each other, and Felipe pointed to the bank and the waters adjacent to it.

There was a gradual slope down to the waters edge, wide enough in extent to accommodate a herd pushing hard to get to the water source. Side by side, they dismounted at the bottom of the slope and surveyed the terrain in all directions.

'Any good signs beyond here, Felipe?'

'Nothin' at all encouragin' Senor Jack. However, this stretch looks as if a herd could swim it, in good conditions.'

'My sentiments exactly.' Jack had made up his mind quite quickly. Uncertainty bothered him, and he was prepared to take a calculated risk. 'Let's get back to the herd. We'll try this spot. Tonight, if we have no delays. What do you say?'

Felipe grinned. 'It would be nice to have them across before night camp, senor. So long as we get back before the leaders smell the water. Shall we go?'

*   *   *

Forty minutes later, Matt Hansen and Ruby Backmann, ahead of the herd and riding with the remuda, encountered the two scouts. Felipe at once resumed his work with the remuda, while Matt and Rudy drew aside for a short further discussion with Jack.

'In the circumstances, I think you're right to aim for a crossin' further west,

Jack. There's no knowin' how much longer that smoke is goin' to blow, an' the fire might keep on comin' this way.'

The eyes of Jack and Matt turned to Rudy. He made a couple of droll expressions with his lined face. 'Me, I see it different. The regular ford is that way. We ain't behind schedule. The wind is bound to turn, or fade away altogether. I say east, but you're the boss, Jack.'

Jack argued and reasoned with his men, and finally stayed with his earlier decision to have the herd swim across at the point chosen.

* * *

The time was after six in the evening when the first groups of beeves came weaving into sight at the top of the gentle slope on the south side of water. Thirty yards back, in timber, on the north side three watching illwishers sharing a spyglass began to enthuse.

Link Thompson flashed his buck

teeth in a wide grin and polished the shiny top of his head with the palm of his hand. 'Well, what do you know? An' who said we was out of luck since we galloped north? Here comes the Circle B herd right to the spot where we're waitin' to renew acquaintance! Hell's bells, if this doesn't give us the chance to get even with Brogan an' that Hansen jasper, I'll eat my old stetson. Take a look through the glass!'

Frenchy grabbed first, hung on for a time, and then Burro confirmed the markings on the beeves and matched Link's enthusiasm.

'Here's what we do. We wait till the herd is headed into the river, till a few score beeves are well over, an' others followin', then we start to shoot into the leaders. Right? That way, we create a mill in the water an' Brogan loses his precious beef. A total disaster, I reckon it'll be. The more I think about this situation, the more I'm convinced the devil is on our side. But we have to do the ambush properly. We spread out, an'

I start the action by firin' on the bell ox. Do you savvy?'

Burro and Frenchy both knew the significance of the bell ox, and they responded unreservedly.

★ ★ ★

Although the hands were tired and in need of a rest, no one demurred when Jack intimated that he wanted to run the beeves across the river before bedding down for the night. They all knew that the wood smoke had made things difficult for them, and the confidence which they had gradually built up for their leader was enough to inspire them to a great effort at the end of a tiring day.

Matt Hansen relinquished duties connected with the remuda, and undertook to be the first across and to keep in close touch with the bell ox while the crucial early moves were made.

More and more groups of long-legged longhorns assembled on the down slope and began to push gently forward. Jack waved his arms, Rudy Backmann did the same on the other flank, and then Matt was urging his mount into the water, only just in time to take the lead from perhaps a score of early pushers and drinkers.

The bell ox was a thirsty beast, but it had the knack of slaking its thirst fairly quickly. Having been tupped in the rear several times and heaved forward by a gathering weight of animals, it gave a last angry bawl of protest and put itself into the stream. Matt was a few yards ahead, and to one side, giving it encouragement. His was a daunting task, but a satisfying one, provided nothing got out of hand.

The ox did as he expected, swimming easily and then strongly. Those beasts which had pushed it from behind were themselves pushed, and so the great transmigration of beeves began. Twenty swimming animals guided by one horse and rider soon became forty, then sixty. And so on. The great swim was on.

Soon there were one hundred beeves in the water, and two hundred more struggling to get water-borne. One man up ahead was joined, further back, by two others. Brogan up the left flank and Backmann on the right. Every man's attention was fully engaged by the drama unfolding, as one thousand animals, a fortune in money, began the hazardous swim. The bell no longer sounded, being under water at the neck of the ox, but the great movement was under way.

★　★　★

Thompson at first could not believe his luck. Even without benefit of the spyglass he could see quite clearly that the rider who had opted to ride and swim first was their old enemy, the man who had spoiled their earlier scheming, Matt Hansen.

What a chance! What an opportunity to eliminate his sworn enemy, in full view of his side-kicks and other enemies who could not get close enough to interfere! His grizzled chin stuck out, accentuating his short upper lip and rodent-like teeth.

'Hey, boys, will you see who that is personally wet nursin' the bell ox? None other than that hombre Matt! Matt Hansen, in the flesh! I wouldn't have missed this opportunity for anythin' in Texas, so help me, I wouldn't!'

His voice, highly pitched and strident, carried quite a long way, but the growing sounds put up by the excited steers more than drowned it in the general cacophony of noise. He settled his rifle in the crotch of a low hanging tree branch, lined up on the leading rider and aimed for the chest.

Fire! Lever, sight, fire!

Some drill out of Thompson's distant past made him do his dirty work with lethal efficiency. For nearly a minute, the results did not seem to matter. On either side of him, another rifle joined in. Every few seconds, a bullet went on its way. Gunshots echoed across the intervening space . . .

Jack Brogan called out too late to warn his closest associate. His voice betrayed his inner agony.

8

Dust upon eddied dust banked up on the southern bank. Steers heaved their way forward, down the slope, pushing other steers ahead of them. A mighty jam of traffic on hooves, downhill on land, into water and across water.

Hit in the chest by the first shot, Matt Hansen lurched in the saddle. At first, he was just trying to avoid spilling into the river, then he was striving to stay wide of the bell ox. Finally, as his senses began to slip away, his vision grew dim and his strength left him. In his last few seconds of life, he knew himself to be a man in the saddle, as he had been since boyhood. The pull of the water made no difference, but his body would not obey his will. He half turned his head, as if to say farewell to Jack, and then he slipped gracefully sideways, his hat still on his head until the scudding waters removed it and accepted him totally.

The sorrel which had carried him so far, for so long, snickered and took in water, unintentionally, for a time losing its sense of direction. Other bullets ripped into the water quite close. The bell ox was disturbed because of the man's disappearance. The sorrel lost its balance, rolled half over and then recovered, going forward again in a panic.

Another bullet struck the extended left horn of the ox, jarring it to the skull, and the great animal responded by turning towards the left, and swimming at an angle to the north shore, no longer certain that it wanted to emerge on that side. Two strongly swimming beeves were hit in vital parts by bullets, immediately losing their rhythm and beginning to sink.

Other animals tried to avoid them, kicking out mightily to make small detours. The confusion in front began to spread.

Over on the left, the next man

furthest forward, Jack Brogan, began to close the gap between himself and the bell ox. He rode like a man possessed, aiming first of all for the sorrel and then realising that his proper quarry was the bell ox. Within two minutes the panicked sorrel crossed ahead of him, nearly colliding with the tired chestnut which had to be chided to keep it on course.

Jack began to think the whole operation was slipping away from him, out of control. He yelled: 'Matt! Matt? Where the hell are you, for goodness' sakes?'

There was no answer, no answer being possible, but the noises around him became clear to his brain once again. The bullets from the timber ahead were being answered by his own men firing from the southern bank. The aim of the ambushers seemed to be concentrated now upon something or things further away.

'What in hell am I doin' here? *What am I doin'?*'

For fleeting seconds, Jack agonised, and then he became aware of the angry cries of his men. None of them was sufficiently clear to be audible, but his brain picked up rather miraculously a piece of advice which came out of nowhere.

'See to the bell ox! Get it under control again, you hear me?'

He nodded, although there was no one to be acknowledged. He hefted a six-gun, but as soon as he surveyed the swimming heaving sea of beeves he holstered it again. Within ten seconds he was within touching distance of the bell ox's damaged horn. The chestnut showed dismay at the closeness of the heavier animal, but Jack leaned out, grabbed the horn and heaved it forward like a boatman working a tiller.

At first, there was opposition: next, the ox turned its head, and then it was back on the original course, headed more or less for the northern bank. Jack coaxed the chestnut to go alongside of the formidable beast. He caught hold of the horn again, but only held it lightly, so that the ox would not turn again into the current.

The ox went ahead, but others behind it needed persuading, too, and as the horse's stamina began to give out, he lost ground with the ox and used his hat to send the follow-up beasts after the leader.

It seemed like an age before the tinny rattle of the ox's bell sounded again on the north shore. The chestnut worked its way out, staggering and shaking itself as the solid earth came up under it. Jack rode forward some fifteen yards. As soon as the first of the substantial trees came up with him, he worked his mount in behind it and turned to survey the rest. Two men had joined Backmann on the far side of the herd. They were working with the segundo to halt the forward rush of the early beeves, seeking to turn them while the effort of swimming still had them winded.

The danger of a mill in the water

seemed to have faded. All shooting appeared to have ceased. Gradually, the steers accepted the coaxing which the riders were imposing upon them. They circled, steaming, as the river water began to dry out on their hides. Some settled, others stood up for a while, but soon it was easier to lie down and rest than to attempt to break out for further exercise. Peace assailed the four-footed longhorns, but not so the horses and riders.

Jack, himself, explored the tree fringe which had hidden the ambush marksmen. It was clear, within a very few minutes, that the three hostile guns had saddled up and moved on. And they had the advantage, for a time. The ambushers' horses were fresh, whereas those of the drovers were near to exhaustion by extra effort during the day, and the tiring swim at the end of it.

Thirty minutes later, the remuda came over without mishap. Nobody really felt like a long ride of vengeance, as they were more or less famished with their late efforts. However, Jack quietly put it about that he was going to ride a mile or two, in search of the ambushers and two men volunteered to take a hand in the search.

Backmann and Felipe Fuente paused beside Jack, wiping down their mounts and rocking their saddles.

'I don't want you to go after the ambushers, Rudy,' Jack replied formally. 'Stay close, if you please. However, you can look around the river banks an' see if there's any sign of Matt's body. Losin' him is likely to haunt me all my days.'

No one this far had mentioned the possible identity of the attackers, but Backmann knew what several of the men were thinking. He busied himself with the men already guarding the herd, and only let his attention wander when the remuda came over, followed by the chuck wagon which was boosted at the four corners by airtight barrels to make it float. On fresh mounts, Jack and Felipe went off in search of the bush-whackers, one riding north-east and the other north-west. They agreed to go no further than two miles so as not to be caught away from the camp by darkness.

Although they rode hard and did not spare themselves, neither of them came within striking distance of the men they sought, even though horse tracks were plentiful.

However, when they returned to the wagon and a belated meal, they found the team in a mean mood, and the reason was not kept from them for very long.

Juan Fuente spoke up. 'Matt's hat has turned up, but there is no sign of his body. But we think we know who attacked us. Pete Rossi, who is always borrowin' my steel to sharpen his knife, he found a coonskin cap hangin' from a branch where the hostile guns were. And there were three sets of initials carved into the back of the tree. L.T., F.D., and B.M. So that about settles it. The same three we had trouble with before, further south. And the fur cap must have belonged to Frenchy. Frenchy Dupont. It had a bullet hole through the top of it. A pity it wasn't on his head at the time.'

'If we ever catch up with those hombres, we'll shoot to kill,' Jack promised.

'We surely will,' the burly cook agreed fervently.

* * *

After that, the tension was back between Rudy Backmann and many of the others. No one doubted that he had been hard at work during the time when the ambush was sprung at the crossing of the Cimarron, but they could not forget that he had been the one to introduce the three renegades to the trail crew on that earlier occasion.

Nicely into Kansas territory, the going became drier. One day, the herd went without water to bed down on. This put the beeves in a fractious mood and gave the night guards a lot of problems. The following day the droving was dodgy in the morning. By mid-afternoon another unlikely phenomenon occurred which made some of the veteran hands believe that their efforts were bewitched. On the near side of a new waterway, excess water — caused by the melting snows of the previous winter — had spilled over the banks of the regular river course and flooded nearly a square mile of low-lying grass with a few inches of water.

This new condition effectively slowed the herd, giving the leaders time to slake their thirst and ease their tired hooves, no doubt, but as more and more beasts moved onto the soggy land a boggy effect began to manifest itself. The first hundred or so of steers were moving almost in slow motion. A situation developed which might have panicked any experienced trail foremen.

At the time of the build up, Brogan was riding wide of the herd on the west side, coaxing the remuda along without too much distance between the horses and the beeves.

Felipe, who was riding point, came back in haste to inform Jack that the soggy earth beyond the steers was clear of bogginess due to a slight upgrade perhaps five hundred yards ahead of them.

'All right, Felipe. I want you to take over my job here! I'll make contact with the boys further east an' see what can be done. We can't have the beasts sinkin' after bringin' them hundreds of miles, can we?'

Before the young Mexican had time to reply, the man riding flank or swing on the east side fired his pistol into the air. His shots were so placed that the other riders received a signal to warn them that a substantial number of beeves were attempting to turn right, or, to go eastward.

Jack shouted an oath. 'I wonder what that's all about?'

'Maybe the grass is firmer on the

right flank, an' the beeves know it, senor!'

Jack checked his spirited mount. 'You sure as hell could be right, amigo, but if they make off in that direction we could lose a day or more, an' I'm not too sure how near the deadline is. One thing I do know, though, if we deliver late the price of every head of beef goes down, an' that Colonel Seth Baron is all businessman since he contracted out of the army, yes sir! I've got to stop a stampede east, an' ease 'em through this bog. Let me think!'

By his side, Felipe sniffed and that gave Jack an idea. He wet his fingers and held them up to check the direction of the light breeze. It was blowing from east to west.

'What are you thinkin' about, Senor Jack?' the Mexican asked anxiously.

'About that wood smoke that gave us so much trouble at the Cimarron, Felipe. Maybe I've got an idea! You get well forward, an' look out for the unexpected, eh?'

148

The other nodded and gave a puzzled grin as the trail boss swung his mount about and cut across the rear of the turgid herd. Jack headed straight for the chuck wagon, and Juan came out to meet him, spreading his hands, his formidable forearms bared.

'What is it, Senor Jack?'

'Have you got the makings of a torch, Juan? The boys on the east flank have trouble, an' I want to try the effect of smoke on the wayward beeves!'

The older Fuente had grave doubts, but he kept his face averted and stayed in the wagon until he had fashioned the makings of a burning brand. He came out to ignite it, and the first reactions came from the mules which pulled the wagon. They put up an unholy row, while one of the rearmost aimed two kicks at the timbers of the box. Juan got back aboard and tackled his own problems while Jack rode east, riding round the rear of the great host of beeves and gradually cutting across to the trouble spot.

Dan Adler, who had fired the gun warning, and his partner, Red Greaves, were having a lot of trouble in holding back beeves growing more aggressive by the second. Dan and his mount were darting forward and withdrawing while the rider flipped his hat within inches of the red eyes of the beeves in an effort to deter them. Greaves was equally energetic, using a big loop of his lariat as a distraction, flipping it and making it crack like a whip.

Both riders appeared to groan with relief as a galloping horse sped into their midst but their thoughts were full of doubts when they took a close look at Jack spurring forward with the lighted torch over his shoulder, acting like some medieval avenger.

'All right, boys, back off a bit an' let me try!'

They complied, and without hesitation Jack waved his torch in the faces of two determined beeves, causing them to flinch and hold back. Further back, other beeves paid little heed, but the determined young rider, his face masked by the grim expression which had become part of his personality on the rugged journey north, was not done; not by any means.

He hauled back on his reins, cautiously switched his hold on the torch and revealed to the other riders that he had attached a lariat to the handle.

'Here we go, then,' Brogan yelled hoarsely.

This was a gamble, if ever there was one. He dropped the torch on the ground, made sure that the grass was not damp enough to put it out, and then started on his stratagem. First he rode backwards some ten yards, dragging the torch. The grass was dry enough to catch fire at once, which was all the rider needed to know. He at once switched his cayuse to face in the opposite direction, and towed the burning brand along the dry spring grass.

All the way along the side of the

bogged down, heaving herd, he rode at a steady pace, dragging the torch. Following him — as he had intended — a low distracting wall of sizzling flame and smoke put a barrier between the beeves and the direction in which they wanted to turn.

As soon as they had recovered from their surprise, Greaves and Adler renewed their efforts to get the beasts on the move again, shooing them away in the original direction required of them. There was a power struggle of sorts for nearly five minutes, during which powerful animals reared up and tried to cross over the backs of their fellows, but gradually the growing weight of beeves on the right flank, harassed by men, flames and a growing pall of smoke which blew in their faces, turned back towards the required course and obstinately worked their way across the troublesome boggy patch.

Jack Brogan's unheard of strategy worked. Due to the checking factor of the boggy ground, a possible stampede into the waters of the river beyond did not materialise.

The whole thousand head of long-horns plodded clear of the watery ground and achieved a walking speed on the slope which led to the river bank. As soon as the leaders on the north side had regained their breath, they started to feed on the new grass. The habit spread. Due to the direction of the wind, which gradually faded but did not change direction, Jack's chancy conflagration failed to become a menace, and the pessimists who were inwardly predicting a difficult night had good reason to realise that they were wrong.

The young trail boss' prestige went up a little further, and one of his exploits went into the memories of his men, to be recounted around camp fires during the rest of the decade.

Jack, himself, was a long time dropping off to sleep under his blanket. He had a vision of his father, Clint, and

Dawn's father, Bert Miller, growing somnolently drunk over a bottle of Scotch whisky, and one or the other of them shaking his head and saying: '*Never, never gamble with a trail herd . . .* '

For a time, Jack was pestered by visions of what might have happened if his trick with the flaming torch had misfired. After that, he turned his tired thoughts to the time taken on the journey and was still unsure of the number of days taken when his mind baulked and he fell asleep.

9

Filbert Rodgers was a big bulky man in his middle forties, tall in the saddle and even taller when he dismounted from his big grey gelding at the scene of the night camp one day later. Although he had been away from Texas for a few years he still favoured a dented side-rolled stetson and a large ornamented forty-pound Texas saddle.

Looking larger than life, with an oiled canvas slicker over his riding gear, he topped six-foot two-inches and his frame carried the muscle to go with it. 'Howdy, folks, I'm Rodgers, Fil Rodgers, foreman an' representative of the rancher who awaits you, Colonel Seth Baron. My partner is Jim Ricks, who does a lot of scoutin' for us on occasion, an' is also real useful when it comes to countin' beeves. Say hello, Jim.'

Ricks was a negro, nearly as tall and possibly ten years older than Rodgers. His hair was thick and white, and his stetson and bandanna both were white in colour, contrasting with the rich dark colour of his skin.

Jack Brogan rose easily to his feet, held his plate away from him and shook the newcomers by the hand. Juan Fuentes and a few of the regulars who were busily eating were also introduced to the newcomers, and the Mexican cook at once put out two helpings of beef stew for the visitors.

Food slowed the conversation, but Jack was assured that he was twenty-four hours inside the time schedule laid down by the colonel when the price per head was fixed at the outset.

After the food, the men started yarning, and the day riders sacrificed some sleep to further acquaintance with the Kansas connection, politely asking about the extent of Colonel Baron's holdings and querying how he intended to build up his herd.

One or two of the main incidents in the journey north were mentioned before the drovers and the visitors slept through till dawn.

* * *

At ten in the morning, the herd approached a bottleneck of rock which Rodgers had prepared the drovers for. The steers were to be counted, ready for the transfer, as they went through the narrows. Rodgers and Ricks were due to take part in the count on behalf of their employer. Nominating two for the Brogans saddened Jack. He had taken Matt Hansen's sorrel into his string of riding horses and he also had in his possession the useful length of knotted rope which had been Matt's device for counting cattle.

'Felipe, I want you to be one of my counters. Do you want the rope?'

The Mexican lad rode over and nodded, smiling broadly. 'Won't you want the rope yourself, Jack?'

Jack shook his head. 'No, I don't want to count. I'm goin' to take a short ride ahead of the herd on this sorrel. Maybe some of Matt's wisdom will rub off on me if I ride nicely. You take the rope, an' Charlie can be your number two. He has the right number of fingers and thumbs, an' the exercise will be good for his grey matter.'

Charlie Brand was the oldest of the regular drovers. At fifty, his hair and chin stubble were grey, but his eyes were bright and he was full of good humour, especially when anyone remarked on his teeth which were scarcely adequate in number to chew Juan Fuente's beef. He accepted the offer, and dismounted long enough to collect a dozen smooth stones. Ten were enough for the job in hand, but a man could drop one or two, if he was careless in shifting them about.

The count started in an atmosphere of good humour, Jack, who was still ill-at-ease on account of Matt's demise, took an early opportunity to ride ahead and be alone.

About fifteen minutes later, he came upon a man on horseback, sitting motionless like an Indian, and did not recognise him until he had spoken. The stranger was a lean, middle-sized muscular individual with a lined forehead, very fair hair and eroded blue eyes. On this occasion he was wearing a pinched in black stetson, a tunic-type shirt of the same colour and a pair of six-guns in what looked like new leather. His facial expression was habitually sullen on account of many years spent on horseback in bright sunlight and dust, and the need to cope with the rigid discipline of life in the army.

'Howdy, Jack, you've changed. I scarcely recognised you. That stetson with the studded band looks like it belongs to another man, an' the folks back home said you were favourin' a chestnut cayuse when you left. I'm Will Hobbs, in case your memory needs boostin'. Left the army a few weeks back with your brother, Roary. We missed you at the outset, but that don't matter.

'Roary, he was keen to settle in on the ranch for a while. Me, I took my discharge differently. I've been ridin' around this way an' that, goin' where I please, for a change, an' actually usin' a white horse, the colour the cavalry said was too conspicuous for the army! Would you believe that?'

Jack removed Matt's stetson, to which Hobbs had referred, and substituted his own. He allowed the sorrel to close with the standing white horse. By leaning out of their saddles, the two men shook hands.

'Good to see you, Will. I suppose my brother sent you after me, if the truth was known. If he did, I'm sorry he felt he had to send someone to hold my hand. I've been doin' all right, you see. Except for an incident or two, setbacks which could have happened to anybody.'

Hobbs backed off a little way. He nodded. 'I brought the sort of messages you'd expect from the family. Dawn Miller's messages are a little different. She sent her love to you an' her Uncle Matt. Do you think I could talk to Matt while the count is goin' on?'

Jack shook his head. His shoulders drooped. He dismounted and signalled for Will to do the same. They found a little shade in the shadow of an old outcrop.

'Will, I'm sorry if I didn't sound too pleased when you showed up. Fact is, Matt is dead. I miss him a lot, he's been like family to me.'

He explained without embellishment how Matt had met his end, and when Will asked the inevitable questions, Jack filled him in on the earlier strife caused by the three renegades introduced by Backmann.

'There must have been quite a few score miles between the spot where you parted with the trio an' the scene of the bush-whackin' at the crossin' of the

Cimarron,' Hobbs commented.

Jack stabbed his cigar towards his listener. 'I know that, but we have proof it was them. There was a coonskin cap an' three sets of initials carved into a tree! We don't have any doubts it was them who shot Matt!'

'I ain't suggestin' they was anyone different, Jack. What occurs to me is that they spent a lot of time comin' by the same route, almost, so they must be full of hate, or something. Otherwise they'd have gone off some place else, long before now. Maybe they'll have made tracks, away from the herd, this time.'

'An' maybe they won't,' Jack argued. 'Who can tell? Anyways, the drovin' is about over. An' since they left us that time, Backmann hasn't made a false move.'

Hobbs nodded, slow to answer. 'You've done well, this trip, Jack. Would you object if I stayed around for a while? I've nearly forgotten how it is to be a cow-puncher, the army has taken up so much of my time. I'd be more use with the remuda than the herd, though. But I keep forgettin' it's almost time to hand over the steers. It don't matter all that much. I won't get in the way. Could be one or two of the hands will know me, or some of my family.'

Jack rose to his feet and stretched. He groaned, but Will made no comment. 'You're welcome, Will. Do what you fancy. It's been a long haul, but I'll be able to relax shortly. Let's go see how the count is comin' along, huh?'

★　★　★

Juan Fuente had assisted the counters by marking down on a sheet of paper every hundred as the counters called out. Jack and Will checked Juan's figures, and when the last steer — one with a slight limp — went through the actual tallying of the score was rapidly achieved.

Fil Rodgers made it one thousand and five.

Felipe Fuente did better. He made it one thousand and eight.

Charlie Brand's tally matched that of Baron's foreman, one thousand and five.

Jim Ricks, the negro, only made it one thousand and three.

Rodgers appeared to be rather formal about the discrepancies. Ricks looked away. The Fuentes and Will Hobbs patiently waited for Jack to suggest a way out of the difficulty. Jack acted a bit sheepish, but he finally did what was expected of him.

'Now see here, boys, Fil's and Charlie's counts were the same. Felipe was a bit above an' Jim was a bit under. How would it be if we did business at the middle figure? Make it one thousand and five, an' all satisfied. What do you say?'

Rodgers' grim dusty face gradually relaxed. 'I'll settle for that. It's the sort of thing the colonel would approve. Okay, then. One thousand an' five head, at twenty dollars apiece. Now, what does that come to?'

The cook was the first to come up with the true answer. 'One thousand head would be twenty thousand dollars exactly, an' the five over the round figure make it another hundred.'

There was a chorus of agreement. After that, all men involved in the count put their signatures on the cook's paper.

Ricks began to whistle, and Rodgers stalked around stiff-legged and anxious to get on with the next part of the business. 'Jack, the colonel is already in town, with the banker. You can collect the payment this afternoon, if you are so minded. Me, I'll stick around here until my team of boys come along from the spread to take over. What do you say about ridin' for town with Jim? He knows his way around, an' he'll introduce you to the Boss.'

'That arrangement suits me fine, Fil. I'll leave my boys here, so that nothin' can go wrong. I'll be back as soon as I can, an' then I'll pay them off. After that, their time is their own, an' so is mine!'

Jack then switched to his own horse, the chestnut, and Jim Ricks' mount was given a rough grooming for the ride into town. Will Hobbs made a show of examining the chestnut admiringly.

'You want I should ride with you, Jack, for company on the way back?'

'It's good of you to offer, Will,' Jack replied cheerfully, 'but that won't be necessary. If you're here when I get back, though, we could have a few drinks an' share a few yarns. After the boys are paid off, that is.'

Hobbs took the refusal with a straight face and promised to stick around.

Jack and Jim made the two hour ride into the town of North Flats without incident. Colonel Seth J. Baron was waiting at the bank as he had promised. The business was transacted with decorum and good manners. When the dealing had been done, the colonel attempted to delay Jack by offering him some hospitality, but Brogan was so keen to have the job finished with and the men paid off that he would only wait long enough to take coffee and make a brief visit to the barber's shop.

At an hour when most fortunate men were putting business aside and thinking of a siesta, he collected his horse and the leather satchel with the herd payment in it and started out for the return ride.

10

Half way to town from the spot on trail where the herd had been counted was an old landmark which had become notorious some twenty years earlier when Kansas achieved statehood. The tall tree known as the Hanging Tree stood about thirty yards north of the worn and eroded track, on the edge of a useful belt of timber which was pitted with buffalo wallows that had appeared much earlier in time.

Hangings were a rough and ready form of justice, and there were various ways in which a man with a rope around his neck was left to end his life because his feet no longer had anything firm under them. This particular place of execution depended for its popularity on the buffalo wallow just a few yards away from the base of the bole. In fact, the wallow had been deepened into a useful pit, and in order to get the victim into position, a long plank was placed across the middle of the pit for the unfortunate fellow to stand on.

In order to despatch the condemned, the plank had to be knocked away. The noose then did its job, and the corpse could be lowered and removed at the convenience of the other parties.

Link Thompson, Frenchy Dupont and Burro McNye, all took a fancy to the spot when they were studying the route from the herd camp to the nearby town. When Jack Brogan and his dark-skinned riding partner went by on the way into town the trio who had plans for the pay-off money were resting amid the timber and deliberately calming themselves so that they would do everything calmly and efficiently when the time came for them to strike.

They were discussing the phenomenon of the negro drover when the rider they were expecting heard their voices from the trail, dismounted and tiptoed up on them and threw a pebble into their midst. At once, the talking stopped and the would-be ambushers dived for their guns. They rolled this way and that, but nothing further happened until Rudy Backmann tossed another pebble at them from behind another tree which they did not have covered.

'Are you hombres figurin' on usin' the hangin' tree for your unfinished business?'

As soon as they heard Backmann's distinctive voice they all relaxed and began to laugh.

Since he lost his fur cap, Frenchy was using a knotted bandanna to protect his head from the sun. He cut short his shrill laughter to answer Backmann's query.

'We did think about it, Rudy, but we don't have a suitable plank for the job, so we had to think again!'

'An' when you thought again, what did you come up with?'

Backmann still had not appeared to them. They became restless, going quiet

170

and peering about from behind their trees to see what he was doing.

'We could make him climb the tree, an' lose his footin' on the hangin' branch,' Burro suggested. 'The fall into the pit would do the trick.'

Backmann made a derisive noise and started towards them, his hands thrust deep into his trouser pockets. 'There was a man in the Bible left in a pit, but he got out again, an' lived a whole lot longer an' he grew rich!'

The other three then stood up and casually moved into view, eyeing each other and talking for effect.

'I guess somebody must have heard him hollerin' an' hauled him out again,' Dupont added thoughtfully.

Backmann turned and tossed another stone into the pit. 'It wasn't like that at all. One of the gang, one of his brothers got cold feet. He hauled him out again, an' sold him to some travellers.'

'We would leave him in the pit, make it look like an accident, if you don't want him found too soon, Rudy.' Link, as usual, sounded more convincing. 'How long do we have before he comes back this way?'

Backmann frowned in concentration. 'Two hours, at least. Maybe longer. Here's what you'll do. Have a snack, take a rest. All right, more rest. Then I'll call you in good time to tool up an' discuss the ambush. Me, I fed myself back at the camp. All I need is a smoke. Oh, an' stay out of sight, in case anyone wanders along the track in between times, an' gets curious.'

* * *

Jack Brogan suffered from the sun as the chestnut which had been with him since San Antonio carried him away from North Flats to fulfil his last act as trail boss of the Circle B herd just sold. For a time, he mused about how many miles he had actually ridden on the back of this horse, but his mind soon tired as the relentless sun dried out the perspiration showing around his shoulders and neck.

The herd money was all in big denomination dollar bills in a fine smooth leather satchel, a gift from Colonel Baron. It swung on his back as he rode like a schoolboy's satchel. As it nudged him, his thoughts went back to those other days which had ended over ten years earlier.

It was time now to think ahead. Just exactly what were his plans? Should he buy a share in some profitable concern in Kansas, or was the best policy a speedy return to his town of origin, and Dawn Miller, his sweetheart? Thoughts of Dawn made him yearn. He was torn between business and resuming his liaison with the girl he always referred to as Sun-up. What a girl!

He could picture her in his mind's eye with absolute clarity. He saw her out riding, frisking and sporting down by the creek: dressed in her Sunday best and turning the heads of the congregation with her classy clothes imported from France, Europe.

It was when he attempted to visualise her in an apron, supervising the running of a busy ranch house that his imagination did not do quite so well. And yet he had seen her often enough, helping her mother, or turning to with sleeves rolled up at spring cleaning time. Maybe he still was not ready for matrimony. Maybe it was himself who was still not quite ready to accept her as a housewife.

One thing he could do, though. He could buy her an engagement ring with some of the money nudging his back. The insistence with which it dug into him constantly reminded him of what a huge amount he was carrying. And conjecture about money reminded him of another matter. Sun-up was not an only child. Apart from Rusty Flood, an orphaned lad adopted by the Millers at the end of the war, she had an older brother. Andrew Miller would be around twenty-six years of age, just a little older than Jack was. From his earliest days, Andrew had been studious. He had made the best of a protracted education, and only disappointed his parents when it became clear that he was not going to take over the Miller ranch after his father.

Andrew liked figures. He favoured going into a bank. So that his father would not be embarrassed locally by having a son working behind a teller's position, he had travelled further north and taken up a position with a banking family operating either in the Oklahoma territory, or in one of the counties of Kansas.

Jack regretted at this stage that he had never taken particular notice about Andrew's present whereabouts. A man with a small fortune in his possession could have benefited through having a friend on hand experienced in the ways of bankers.

Very gradually, Jack's alertness went back upon him. He had with him a small flat bottle of whisky, but he decided that hard liquor was not the sort of drink to quench his thirst, and that it might render him less wide awake than before.

He drank water from his canteen, but it was warm, brackish almost and it did not help him bear up under the oppressive sun. He lighted a small cigar, smoked a half of it and threw away the rubbed-out butt. After that, he just aimed to stay awake and see the miles go by. The sun was over his left shoulder, and over the top of the timber which broke the sky line.

He blinked hard, and brushed salt sweat out of his eyes, thinking there was perhaps something special about the trees in question, but the sudden cacophony of sound took him entirely by surprise. The crackle of rifle fire, more than one rifle — two or three! Bullets came at him from both sides of the trail. He braced himself to feel the impact of lead, but somehow the bullets were not on target. They ripped into the track around the hind legs of the chestnut and a little way behind it.

The startled beast whinnied and leapt forward, speeding up to avoid the new menace. Within two or three strides, the second surprise occurred. A lariat, which had been concealed by dust and carefully assembled small stones, suddenly became taut about a foot above the trail. The chestnut failed to react swiftly enough. The lariat whipped its legs from under it and rolled it heavily and hurtfully in the dust and eroded stones.

A steadying hand on the money satchel cost Jack a useful second or two, as he pitched forward, sailing through the air with his arms belatedly coming up to protect him from the earth on impact.

The chestnut did a painful somersault, a lurch and recovered itself, to gallop on unattended, while Brogan's head slithered a short way, protected by his stetson and then connected with an unyielding boulder. As his senses left him, he was starting to hear the distinctive sounds of riding boots on gritty earth, and a derisive bitter laugh which was very familiar and might have come out of a nightmare.

* * *

'Never mind the horse, pick him up an' get him up there by the pit,' Backmann instructed forthrightly.

'Sure you can manage to carry that money bag unaided, Rudy?' Dupont queried, as he bent over the inert body.

He was reminded not to push his luck as the trio hefted the victim off the track and carried him, as had been suggested. No one came along to interrupt their efforts. Brogan's mouth was sealed with a bandanna, and a sleeve of sack cloth was pulled down over his face, so that he was in grey darkness as well as having his mouth sealed. Within five minutes, he was lowered into the depths of the pit under the hanging tree, and there he began to stir, pulling slowly against his bonds some little time after his attackers had left.

* * *

Life was a black void. No light, no sound, no room to move. Nothing. Only a singing in the ears. After a short time, small bruises and cuts began to ache. After that, pains brought on by tight ropes tugging and straining against his muscles and flesh.

Jack's temperature must have risen because the beads of perspiration on his brow multiplied. His leaking pores appeared to be all working against him. The whole of his head down to neck level, and then on, down his chest: inside his belt. Discomfort to a high degree and no signs whatever of a let up. No relief.

A few gentle tugs on the trussing ropes which secured his ankles and wrists and held him like a semi-taut bow did nothing to improve matters, but they did confirm the seriousness of his position.

The blackness. Lights started to come and go behind his eyes. The only light he was aware of. If he kept still, his ears functioned.

He started a series of small moves, using up energy at a critical rate, but he felt that his time was running short. One part of his mind told him what had happened to him. He had been ambushed very thoroughly by enemies who knew what they were about. His mount had been startled, and a rope had brought about his downfall. Knocked unconscious, he had been moved from the scene of the trail to some spot less obvious.

Whoever had done it, had left him for a slow death. The raucous laughter had been that of Rudy Backmann, the trail foreman whom he had deposed. Backmann and others. What others? Thompson and company had spent a lot of time keeping in secret touch with the herd. Why not them?

Why hadn't they put bullets through him instead of using lead to humble him? Could hate make them leave him to die slowly? Did road agents behave rationally? Did it matter to them whether a man died slowly and painfully, or would they cease to think about their victim as soon as he was out of their sight?

After travelling for a yard or so with his arched back touching a wall of earth, he gave up the effort. One last kick brought him in contact with a hard metallic object, on the ground. He tried to get a hold of it, but it slithered away . . .

His hopes of survival faded with it.

* * *

Will Hobbs heard the muted sound of gunshots from over a mile away. Instinct, more than anything else, made him ride out from camp to meet the returning trail boss, against the latter's wishes.

The shots roused him from a restful position behind a rock on the north side of the trail, where he had been taking life easy and keeping out of the heat. He took a minute or two to tighten up his saddle and swing into it, and after that he was fully alert.

No jack rabbit ever merited a flurry of rifle shots. There had been some sort of ambush a short distance nearer to town. If he was not too late, he could find the scene of the incident and perhaps give aid to the underdog. Jack Brogan was the obvious victim. A man with a pay roll and no back-up guns to protect him.

The startled chestnut was still running when Will spotted it. Nerves made it turn off trail and run up a rock fault, a gully of sorts, which was its undoing. The gully narrowed, and the unfortunate beast was trapped, scarcely able to move at all.

Will came up behind it, aware that fleeting minutes were slipping away during which a man's life might be forfeit. He forced himself into the patient role necessary to get the chestnut out again. Five minutes lost. And then he was heading back for the trail, all his senses alert, wary for another ambush.

None came. No signs of life. At the spot where the lariat had been used, the chestnut reacted in such a way that Hobbs was warned. He stopped, still watchful, and made a careful examination of trail and the earth on either side. The district was strange to him, but he saw the branch lacking bark on the old hanging tree, and there and then he began to reconstruct the recent ambush.

Five minutes later, he was down in the pit, releasing the sorry figure he had thought to be dead. Jack's face was an unhealthy colour due to the effort he had been forced to make to keep breathing effectively.

Brogan's mouth was bruised, his eyes ached with the brightness of sunlight, which he had not expected to experience again. His wrists and ankles shook as they were freed. The victim acted as if he had a touch of the ague. Hobbs braced him against his knee and his head lolled against the earth wall.

Jack's eyes followed Will's as the latter noticed the revolver a few feet away. That was the object Jack had felt and lost. Will surmised that it would have one bullet in it, a means of suicide, rather than something to aid an escape. He was right. The water tasted warm, almost bitter to Jack and yet he was able to swallow it.

Although he was humiliated, he had survived through the stubbornness of one man, a friend of his brother's. Everything had gone so well. Too well. In allowing himself to be robbed before he paid his men, he had fallen at the last hurdle, the last obstacle.

Jack murmured: 'Why did you do it, Will? After I put you off, why did you come lookin' for me?'

Hobbs gave a wry grin. 'Not because you endeared yourself to me, Jack. Because I owed a couple of favours to your brother. He eased me out of tight situations twice. Once when Indians out of a reservation cornered me, and another time when white renegades ambushin' a pay train took me as hostage. Welcome back to the land of the livin'. I guess you've lost everything except what you stand up in, an' your horse, which more or less blundered into me. What do you plan to do, right now?'

'I wish I knew, Will, but right now I'm frustrated, boilin' up with anger, spoilin' for revenge! I don't know what to do first! Before I passed out, back there on the trail I could swear I heard that raucous mockin' laughter belongin' to Rudy Backmann, but I don't suppose I could prove it. The boys back there at the camp, they're waitin' for their pay, an' I don't have it. I'd give anythin' not to have to go back there an' admit it to them!'

Will cleared his throat. 'You might be interested to know Backmann rode out of camp before I did. I think he's always had it in for you. Still, my opinion ain't much help. Tell you what I'll do. I have a roll of cash with me. I'll go back an'

185

pay off the hands for you, if you like. You can square up with me later.'

Jack stopped pacing and considered the offer.

'But surely it would need the best part of a thousand dollars, Will. You wouldn't carry that amount around with you?'

Hobbs chuckled. 'These here lined tunic shirts are very useful for travellin' gents.' He ran his hands around his tunic, back and front, and managed to raise a slight crackle, as if paper was concealed within it. 'I have that amount, an' I do have other means of raisin' further dough. So do you want me to pay the hands, or do I come along with you an' make the acquaintance of the ambushers?'

Jack shook his head, and hunkered down. 'I don't know what the chances are of catchin' up with the ambushers, Will. I believe I ought to look for clues in town, but they'd be fools to be hangin' around waitin' for trouble, don't you think? What what would you do if Backmann had returned to the camp site?'

Hobbs became quite still for three seconds. Then he pulled his two revolvers simultaneously. Jack blinked hard and sprang to his feet.

'I'd challenge him, amigo, an' see what sort of a reaction he'd give! But I don't think he'll turn up that easily. Even if he was guilty he wouldn't have the pay money with him, either. I'll go an' pay off the hands, like I suggested. Then I'll ride back into town an' look for signs of you. If you require back-up, I'll provide it. If you've moved on, I'll think of something else to do. Now, let's get out of this hole before we get too used to it. I'll go first.'

One after the other, they scrambled up the rope which had been used by Will to make the descent. On the upper level, Hobbs kept Jack talking. The delay gave him time for his eyes to adjust and for his mind to size up some of the problems which he was intending to face alone. Fortunately, the chestnut had not suffered any bad sprains. The revolver left in the pit turned out to be Jack's own. His fingers were a little nervous as he filled up the empty chambers with some of Will's ammunition.

Presently, they were mounted up.

'What shall I tell the boys?'

Jack scowled. 'I leave that to you. I may have learned a lot about cow handlin' but I'm short on wisdom. I'd like the chance to put my own house in order, but I don't have a lot of confidence in what lies ahead of me. I feel that my past is a big zero, an' the future is uncertain, so we'll have to see. Adios, amigo, an' thanks for everything.'

They shook hands briefly, looked one another directly in the eye, and parted.

Jack had the right slant on his own future. As he rode towards North Flats for the second time, his mind kept slipping back to San Antonio. He had glimpses of his parents, and folks who were always around the area he knew so well. Sun-up, in her many gay frivolous moods. And the workers at the ranch. Even Zeke, the blacksmith, and Ah Feng, the second cook, had a more secure future than he himself appeared to have.

11

Even after two hours in the saddle, Jack Brogan was raging inwardly about the way in which he had been robbed. He was also raging outwardly on account of a build up of thirst, which kept from him his need to eat. In attempting to deal with the thirst first, he succeeded in that one respect, but his anger burned into words and tended to put off anyone near to him to whom he put pertinent questions about his enemies.

As was customary in western towns, the locals were wary of a man who rode in with a whole battery of questions to ask who claimed he had been robbed. They listened, shook their heads and moved away, wondering who had heard them being questioned.

Jack visited three saloons. In each of them, the green baize top of card tables attracted him, but he kept clear and worked hard to focus on faces. He asked one fellow where the Baron ranch was, but the stranger was not attracted to him and the details of the route were deliberately misguiding.

Tom 'Banjo' Ritts, the town marshal, could have made a good spy. He had the talent to blend into backgrounds or groups of people without anyone witnessing his arrival. From three tables away, in the third saloon, Ritts (who had once made a name for himself by using a banjo as a club) witnessed Jack's condition and overheard the type of questions he was asking. As he did not want to be grabbed and harangued, the marshal looked away, kept his arm and derby hat hiding his drooping black moustache from those who knew him, and sidled out unnoticed to another tavern before Jack's deteriorating condition embarrassed him.

Some time later, Jack lurched out at the back, in search of the toilet, and lost his way. On open ground at the rear of the saloon, he succumbed to a growing tiredness, placed his back against a fence and allowed his head to droop onto his chest. The sun made considerable progress in its daily journey towards the west while he was in that position.

Two hours later, a peace keeper of a different type noticed his drooping chestnut horse in an isolated position at the saloon hitchrail. Zack Placer, the constable, studied its lines and decided that if its owner knew its value, he had to be a man of means. He moved into the Totem Pole saloon, drank the tall glass of beer already poured out for him at the end of the long bar, and used his eroded grey eyes on the customers. Placer was forty-five: tall, lean, with a shock of grey hair and a walrus moustache totally hiding his wide thin mouth.

Five minutes later, he was leaning over the sleeping figure out at the back. The first thing he noticed was a few dollar bills folded into a shirt pocket. He was impressed. Jack flinched as the constable touched his shoulder.

'Evenin' amigo, are you lookin' for a place to sleep? This here ain't one of the best. In fact it ain't allowed. Do you have a chestnut horse waitin' for you some place?'

Jack made a big effort to recover his faculties. He nodded. 'How much do you charge for a night in the hoosegow?'

He attempted a big belly laugh, but his stomach merely flapped and left him feeling uncomfortable.

'The marshal has slidin' scales of pay for that sort of thing. Kind of expensive. I could help you to a less costly spot for the night, stable your horse, as well, if you want a little help. What do you say?'

Jack blew out his cheeks. He had a feeling that the fellow talking to him from behind the moustache was genuine enough, but his thoughts were addled. He reached into his shirt pocket, pulled out the dollar bills and promptly dropped them. Placer retrieved them, and helped him to his feet. Brogan had no recollection of being helped across the vacant lots, or of arriving in the rooming house of Mrs Millie Drew, a big plump friend of the constable's who had a shrewd eye to business.

However, that was what happened to the young Texan that evening. He was too far gone to do justice to the evening meal and, that being so, he was put to bed where he slept through to the following morning.

Later, after a good breakfast, he talked with the woman, Mrs Drew. Her sunburn was so good that she had to have a touch of negro blood in her, perhaps two generations earlier. However, she was a shrewd woman and on occasion she would help a roomer, provided he interested her. Jack gave her an idea of what had caused his difficulties. She asked him if he thought his buyer, Colonel Baron, was keen enough to send his men after the pay roll to take it back again by force. This suggestion shocked Jack, whose reactions to such a possibility came through quite clearly.

There was further discussion.

Eventually, Millie Drew had heard enough. With her substantial forearms folded across her Junoesque bosom, she made her pronouncement.

'All righty, Mr Brogan. You've described to me the appearance of four men you are keen to meet. I'll put the word around. If you're still enjoyin' my hospitality an' I hear of them, I'll let you know. All right? Now, off you go. Circulate yourself around the town, in case the folks get to wonderin' what you're doin' on my establishment.'

Still not quite broke, Jack touched his hat to her, and sauntered off. He checked that the chestnut was in the livery which Constable Placer had mentioned, actually went looking for the constable, so that he could thank him, and then moved on again, having been informed that no one answering the description of the men he sought were to be found on the reward notices in the local peace office.

North Flats did not have a lot of surprises for a man who did not really want to be there. Jack sauntered on until he came to a meadow on the south side of town where fairs and markets were wont to be held. This day was not a special one, but the one semi-permanent marquee was open and there he had his first surprise.

There were no merchants in there: only gamblers. Men with cards, dice, and roulette wheels. All the sort of people whose company he could well do without in his present state of funding. The old inate drawing power of the gamble, nevertheless, made him stroll around inside, and there he met with a familiar figure.

★   ★   ★

Will Hobbs had arrived back in town the previous evening, not staying with the trail crew for very long. By the time he arrived Constable Placer had removed the striking chestnut from the hitchrail, and Jack's presence had remained a mystery, following a brief search of the saloons.

Will had risen at an early hour and strolled about the town fully on the alert at a time when road agents and others were as sleepy as anyone else. The streets of North Flats had not rendered up anyone answering to the description of Backmann or his three sidekicks.

The pull of the gambling tent had then served the ex-cavalryman as a place to get his bearings and to win for himself some funds to replenish his stock after advancing the sizeable loan for the trail drovers' wages. He had tried to set up a game where men could shoot at a number of playing cards nailed to a board. That had been ruled out by Marshal Ritts, on account of gunshots disturbing sensitive members of the general public.

Next, he tried a set of darts, but a big

rumbustious visitor had complained that the darts were not flighted properly, favouring the firm.

Once again, he failed to cause a rumpus. After strolling round again until the anti-element had left, he started to play *find the lady* with a deck of cards. This soon drew a coterie of clients around him. He started to win, after losing sufficiently to get his audience keen. In an hour, he made fifty dollars.

His success annoyed the regular professional stall holders and three of them strolled over to put the views of all the rest, during a lull.

'It ain't considered fair for a stranger to set up in card gamblin' when there's another person already workin' the cards. We'd like to ask you to desist.'

The bulky fellow stepped back. Will followed his eyes. In the doorway, a couple of seedy-looking drifters were waiting with their hands on their belts.

Will laughed. 'Well, who was it said it wasn't fair? The state governor?'

Will stepped half a pace backwards, as if he was non-plussed. In a flash, he executed a double draw of the smart matched six-guns he had bought with some of his discharge money. He tossed them in the air, caught them in opposite hands, rolled them on the trigger guard and slipped them back in the holsters. The fellow who had addressed him was about to protest, but at that moment a hornet flew into the marquee. Will's quick ears picked up its winging sound. He drew one revolver, shot it accurately in an upward trajectory, and holed the canvas of the building.

'All right, gents, here's what I'll do. When I start up again, I'll be usin' thimbles, right? Instead of findin' the lady, my clients will be tryin' to trace a pea under three thimbles. Now, how will that suit?'

He did not wait for them to pass judgement on him. Instead, he produced the fifty dollars he had collected and presented each of the three members of the deputation with ten dollars.

'I'd like you to accept this money on behalf of the local gamblin' association. After that, no more objections, otherwise I'll have to complain to the colonel, the officer commandin' my old regiment. No hard feelings, pickings for all. Adios, gents.'

The trio nodded gravely and backed off. A deputy marshal came to see what the shooting was about, and the two troubleshooters by the door explained it away as a fellow disposing of a nuisance.

★   ★   ★

Jack hovered a few yards away, embarrassed to see his ally gambling for an income. Will was far more at ease. He drew Jack over and arranged an exchange of information while the two of them went through the motions of the thimble rigging.

Will fixed it for Jack to win several

times. When he had collected ten dollars, Hobbs packed up his profitable sideline and strolled out with Jack for a meal. They ate and drank, discussed Jack's dilemma from all angles, and finally parted. Will intimated that he would be around for a day or two, and Jack promised to get in touch with him if he had anything positive in the way of information.

The two of them could so easily have become inseparable friends. They could have stayed together, but Jack's appalling loss of funds had driven him into himself and made him feel guilty about accepting handouts from Will. The latter perceived his inward torments and did nothing to aggravate them.

That evening, they took a few drinks together. At a reasonable hour, Jack decided to turn in, and Will walked him as far as Millie Drew's house before parting company. As soon as Will had gone away, Jack retraced his steps to the centre, ambled into another saloon and began to regale himself with whisky.

He managed to stop himself before he passed out, and somehow he found his way back to the rooming house without incident. Millie checked that he was stripped off and in bed, and thought no more about him.

At breakfast, he was suddenly thinking about the chestnut, and the warning he had received that it would be turned out of the livery after twenty-four hours if no further payment had been made. Jack suddenly wanted to be on its back. He walked and ran all the way to the livery, but he was too late.

The chestnut had been taken away at an early hour the previous evening: in fact, at the time when all overnight horses were bedded down in the stalls for the night. Jack was upset, and angry, but the forthright and confident owner of the stable believed that he was altogether within his rights.

A growing feeling of foreboding haunted him as he raced across town to the meadow where the gambling marquee stood. At the rear side of the marquee, the town had erected for itself a small pole corral for general use. A single glance showed that the chestnut was not in the corral, the location stated by the ostler. Jack began to tear himself apart inwardly. Anger, frustration and a certain sickness born of self-depredation and loathing gripped him and made him feel utterly useless.

His breath became harsh, and he knew that he was not doing himself any good. In order to regulate his conflicting emotions, he went for a walk round the perimeter of the meadow. And his luck changed, as a result. In a tiny copse, just a few yards away from the corral he caught a glimpse of movement. A horse. *His* horse. The chestnut was pegged out inside the ring of trees. It was cropping grass, and generally taking life easily, and yet it was slightly restless. As if it did not know its future, Jack decided.

His first inclination was to dash over to the copse and show the cayuse a good deal of his relief about the two of them being together again. Something held him back. The horse had not been placed in the corral; or, if it had, someone had moved it out again.

Some other party had an abiding interest in J.B.'s chestnut, the horse he had brought all the way from southern Texas. But who was it? Someone connected with his previous setback, or just an ordinary thief?

He decided to postpone his union with the animal, long enough to give an unknown stranger time to appear. Accordingly, he squatted down just wide of the corral, and began to smoke a small cigar while he kept watch on the copse and the horse.

Some ten minutes later, a stranger entered the meadow, strolled in the direction of the marquee. Only one or two locals were in the big tent, and they were not really interested in early gamblers. The stranger moved into the tent, came out again and used his eyes to examine the lie of the land, and any possible strollers who could interfere with his plans.

Jack's interest in the fellow grew. Two things were unusual about him. The hat he wore had its brim clipped upright on one side in the Australian mode. On one shoulder he carried a saddle and on the other horse jewelry. The sight of that saddle fixed Jack's attention exclusively on him. He was around forty years of age, with dark hair and sideburns. His cheeks had a hollow look to them. Close set green eyes encroached on a thick Roman nose. A leather vest topped his black shirt and partially concealed his gun belt which was well weighted with hardware.

After that, Jack sucked gently on his cigar, awaiting the coming together of the shifty Australian and the cropping chestnut horse. His patience was fully restored. So far as he knew, he had never seen this fellow in his life. Chance was bringing them together. Jack knew a horse thief, and he had suffered too much in the way of humiliation to go easy on this fellow.

Inevitably, the fellow slipped by the corral and ghosted into the trees. The rigging of the blanket and the saddle was a leisurely affair. Jack marvelled about that. Perhaps the thieving galoot was afraid of spooking the animal.

Jack moved up, slowly and with a good deal of cunning. The thief was so absorbed in what he was doing that he failed to notice the stealthy approach, even when the chestnut whinnied. Jack shifted nearer, one tree at once, and he jumped just as the fellow was about to put his foot in the stirrup.

The stranger was off balance. Jack clouted him on the side of his head, knocked off his unusual headgear and sent him slithering earthwards. The stranger landed on his knees, shuffled sideways, thought about a verbal protest and decided that there was no percentage in such a move. He tried a couple of open-handed gestures as he rose to his feet, to no avail.

They sparred. Jack danced forward, looked as if he was going to do some head butting, but at the last second he straightened up, used a knee to wind his opponent and executed a swift one-two on the other's face. The thief fell backwards, pivoted awkwardly about and made as if to run off. In fact, he collided with a tree bole and did himself no good at all.

Jack closed with him, glancing as he did so to see how the chestnut was making out. The encounter had disturbed it a little, but it had merely shifted its position a few yards and was patiently awaiting the outcome. Wary of hitting the tree with his fist, the young Texan then closed with his adversary and pulled and pushed and punched him this way and that until they were both off balance and thoroughly out of breath. They rolled on the grass, striving for an advantage and not finding one with any ease.

'Hold on, hold it, amigo,' the Australian begged. 'This, this horse, I had a special reason for borrowin' him.'

Jack closed his working mouth with a

hasty punch. 'The hell you had! I've been robbed before this week, an' no sort of an excuse is goin' to help you, amigo!'

Jack hit him again, drawing blood from the mouth. Under the fellow's head a rock stuck out of the earth. The Texan used it to advantage, beating the thief's head repeatedly upon it.

'Land's sakes, gimme a break, will you? I can show you some easy money — a lot of money . . . '

'Do you make your own?' Jack mocked. 'How much money?'

'Hun . . . hundreds, maybe a thousand, or two!'

The idea of suddenly recouping himself went through Jack's fuddled thoughts and was of interest. He eased up, kicked his gun and the other fellow's pair further away from the two of them, and sucked in air. His breathing eased.

'What's my horse got to do with this easy money?'

'It was needed, for a robbery. One

already planned.'

Jack thought about a robbery. He had been robbed. Why not rob someone else, refurbish himself? Get his own back. The law of Moses, was it? Well, maybe not quite that. No, a different law, then. He found his curiosity growing.

12

Humbert Price, the tall conspirator with the closely-trimmed black beard, paced up and down, acting like an office manager dictating to a subordinate.

' . . . so you see, Jack, the three of us are professionals. Not only do we dress up like city gents to do our heistin' but we plan our work down to the last detail. For instance, unlike most bank robbers, we hold off for a whole month after doin' a job. Moreover, we always cross a border into another county before we strike again.

'That sort of plannin' pays off. We do the inside work. Occasionally, we use someone like you or your friend to help out in other ways.'

'What other ways did you have in mind, Humbert?' Jack asked casually.

Bluey O'Dowell, the Australian who had attempted to steal the chestnut, had arranged this meeting. It was taking place in a secluded strip of land about one and a half miles west of North Flats. The time was a little after ten in the morning, on the following day after Jack and Bluey had met.

Humbert Price, Ace Pullar and Ben Creviss were alike and yet not alike. Price was tall, and talked like a professor, although he was more a con artist than a learned man. Ace Pullar was medium-sized and lightly built: an ex-gambler, and a bit of a dandy, dressed in a tall pinched-in black stetson, a dark jacket over a checkered waistcoat. His upper lip wore a thin brown line of moustache, trimmed close like the diamond of hair on his pointed chin. Ben Creviss was short and broad. A former gun salesman, he sported a brown suit, a short lush moustache and a tall cream-coloured undented stetson.

They all smoked cigars and each of them wore a six-gun at the waist.

'Oh, lookin' after the ridin' stock.

Coverin' our back trail on the way out. That sort of thing. Ace thought that stealin' a horse or two would be cheaper than hirin' or exchangin' but Bluey there didn't make out well as a horse thief. Never mind. No great harm has been done. So far, we haven't heard a lot from the friend you introduced, Jack. Perhaps he would be kind enough to say whether he will join us before we give out with more details.'

All eyes turned towards Will Hobbs, who was sitting on a log cleaning a revolver with a piece of rag. Jack's curiosity about Will was as intense as that of any of the others. He had always understood Will to be scrupulously honest. In fact, Hobbs' acceptance of the offer to come to the meeting had rocked Jack at the outset.

Will cleared his throat and spat tobacco juice onto the grass.

'My buddy, Jack, is an expert with horses. I'd back him against any of you. Me, I'm an artist with guns. Yer, count me in. I'll back up Jack in horse handlin' an' guard the retreat. How will that be?'

Humbert, Ace and Ben studied each other's faces. Eventually they all nodded. 'All right, then, you Jack an' your friend, Will, are in business. Now, listen carefully. We go to work at noon tomorrow. Our strike is against the Flats District Banking Company in West Flats, a few miles north-west of here.'

He talked for nearly five minutes and then paused. His mind was ordered and he gave clear instructions.

'Now, anyone with a query?'

Bluey, in particular, looked vague at the word 'query' but no one had any questions to ask.

'Anyone havin' second thoughts, then?'

Will broke the silence. 'Not second thoughts, but I once got into a spot of bother in West Flats. Before I joined the army. So, if you don't spot me before the event rest assured I shall be checking out for familiar faces among peace officers, an' lyin' low.'

Price asked Will a few questions, which were answered to his satisfaction. The meeting broke up some ten minutes later, and the conspirators split up into two groups and left separately.

★ ★ ★

Jack Brogan and Will Hobbs made contact with Bluey around seven in the morning. They came together near a livery, made a bit of small talk and then rode off in the direction of West Flats at a steady pace. The last four hundred yards into the town which was three miles away turned out to be a downgrade. Unconsciously, horses and men became a little more keen and Jack and Bluey were slightly surprised when Will, riding in the middle of them, slowed up his mount and cleared his throat.

'Right, fellows, you all know the drill from what was said yesterday. I'm droppin' out right now. Don't get worried about what I'll be doin'. I have my own methods of preparin' for an illegal shindig like this one. You two carry on, hitch up, take breakfast an' take a look round you-know-where. Follow the instructions, an' don't do anything to complicate things.'

Jack was shaken when Will moved away. He had not realised how much he had been depending upon the ex-soldier for moral support. Now, it was born in upon him what he was doing. He, Jack Henry Brogan, was actually preparing to rob a bank, to make up for what he had lost at the hands of desperadoes. Two wrongs to make things right. Will Hobbs drawn into an affair which could turn sour. Jack's own great wilful fling in search of total freedom, it could all turn sour for him, too. He shuddered at the thought of being on the wrong side of bars: worse still breaking down rocks in a penitentiary. *What the hell . . .*

Bluey's phenomenal appetite carried Jack through a short period of near despair. After the meal, they sauntered past the bank, approached it from the rear angle, and generally savoured the atmosphere. As they came away, they cast a few backward glances. Jack felt himself studying the ordinary everyday happenings. The strolling gossips, the idlers who sat on sidewalk benches and smoked. The women with their shopping baskets. The shopkeepers and shoppers. A strolling deputy with a shotgun and a word for everybody.

Automatically, the couple speeded up. Jack grabbed Bluey's arm.

'Hey, hombre, what do bank robbers do before the big event?'

Bluey stopped biting his finger nails, stared into Jack's face from close-up, and shook his head. 'Hey, Brogan, you ain't so smart as I thought you were. Why, they take a few fingers of whisky. Not enough to fuddle the brain, but enough to calm the nerves. Understood?'

★   ★   ★

High noon. Price, Pullar and Creviss walked into the front of the bank, one after the other, all carrying leather bags not unlike the doctor's traditional bag. Needless to say, the bags were empty. Not so the chambers of the discreetly worn six-guns.

Ordinary business was being transacted by a young teller, a somewhat older teller and the veteran president, who was in his dotage. The long counter ran from the front to the rear, down the right hand side of the room. The two tellers operated at the grilles, whereas the old president merely graced the place in a rocking chair strategically placed in a corner near the front wall.

Over on the left were chairs, for the comfort of clients. A plump Junoesque travelling woman, overdressed for the time and the place, was fanning herself with a silk handkerchief. The other two customers were male, and men accustomed to travelling. One of them came away from a grille, pocketed a wad of notes and sauntered over to where the other one was squinting up at a map of the county pinned on the wall.

Humbert Price cleared his throat, and that started the action. He moved over to the counter, pulled a large green handkerchief from his pocket and glanced at his colleagues. Ace Pullar crossed over to confront the older of the two tellers at the second grille, while Ben Creviss gave his attention to the other customers.

Acting with the precision born of practice, the trio all masked up with their green handkerchieves. Within seconds they had all pulled their guns, two at the grilles and one overlooking the customers.

'Lady and gents, this is a stick-up as you can see,' Creviss remarked conversationally. 'However, there's no need for any of you to get in a sweat, unless you are lookin' for trouble. Here, hold this.'

The small man handed over his cigar to the man who had drawn money, and the fellow took it with a trembling hand. The other man raised his hands above his head while the breathless woman struggled to clip her pince-nez on her nose. In the meantime, Price and Pullar made clear their needs, pointing out the bills of large denomination, visible in the drawers of the large wall safe, which was open.

The president stopped rocking. His eyes watered, his body looked as if he was in the grip of ague. Creviss kicked his hold-all across the floor towards Pullar, and at the same time waved his hand at the window facing onto the street. Outside, Bluey O'Dowell saw the signal. He whistled long and loudly.

The woman fixed her pince-nez, scared herself to death by taking in what she saw, and promptly fainted. Her ample body slowly slid to the floor and distracted all parties for a few seconds.

★　★　★

Hearing the whistle without difficulty, Jack Brogan, at the rear, entered the building by a single door on that side which gave access to the president's private den behind the trading room. Jack had all the horses lined up and ready at a hitchrail behind the mail office building next door. Only in the few minutes immediately prior to noon had he shown any signs of nerves. Now, he was perspiring steadily: wondering where Will Hobbs had got to and what was likely to happen if anyone started shooting, or gave the alarm.

The president's office had an atmosphere all its own. A monster of a desk took up a goodly portion of the room, along with some filing cabinets and a corner safe. Partitioned off on the right was a small room. A dripping sound suggested a wash room.

Jack stood behind the desk, wondering exactly what was going on in the main part of the building. His white bandanna slipped off his face. He fixed it again. A slight noise alerted him. He crossed to the wash room, threw open the door and found himself face to face with the younger of the two tellers, who had sneaked out from behind the counter by a communicating door. Jack pointed his revolver at the teller, who slowly raised his hands and began to breathe more deeply through excitement. Using the gun as an indicator, Jack ordered the young man across to the door which linked the private office with the main section.

As the door was opened by his prisoner, there was uproar beyond it.

Price was shouting. 'Where the hell did that young teller go?'

At the same time, the old president — overlooked this far on account of his apparent senility — threw a heavy ear trumpet through the glass of the window behind him and thereby started the alarm. The three money bags were loaded and had been taken off the counter by Pullar. As the window glass shattered, the older balding teller stepped on a rope near his feet behind the grille. A revolver in a fixed position then fired through the wooden panel which separated his legs from those of anyone in the client's position. The bullet passed between the legs of Ace Pullar who almost fell over backwards with the shock.

In the street, Bluey shot out the other window by way of a diversion just as the younger teller was propelled into the room from behind. The teller in question was a tall, lean, bespectacled young fellow with neat fair hair and a trimmed beard of the same colour.

'So there he is!' Price shouted, behind his mask. 'Shoot him, why don't you?'

Judging by the noises made by Creviss and Pullar, they too approved the idea of shooting the young teller. Someone shouted in the street. Jack, therefore, fired two bullets through the front door to dissuade anyone bent on a rush. He then gestured to his partners, who went through into the rear, leaving him to deal with his prisoner. As the last of the trio disappeared from view, the fair young man started to turn round to face the person menacing him. On impulse, Jack gave him a sharp clip alongside of the head with the gun barrel and was thankful when he slid to the floor.

As he followed the other three through into the rear, he murmured: 'For goodness' sake, stay down, Andy!'

And then he scuttled after his partners, slamming the door behind him.

13

Always a flurry of shots in a busy town create a commotion. This high noon incident in West Flats was no exception. Men and women came from all directions, puffing with exertion to try and see where the shooting was, and who was doing it. However, they were slow to gather . . .

Bluey O'Dowell, having created a diversion and fired a shot or two, departed abruptly for other parts, going first towards the west and then turning south through two alleyways, before cautiously mounting his skewbald horse and slowly edging his way out of town towards the west. Unknown to Jack Brogan, a separate bargain had been struck between the three leading conspirators and the Australian. He had been paid a sum of fifty dollars to carry out his little diversion and make sure no one rushed the front of the building before the intruders got clear.

The horses belonging to the trio were in tiptop condition. Moreover, Jack had checked them over less than half an hour before the actual assault on the bank. Price, Pullar and Creviss rode hard towards the east, every now and then turning to look behind them in order to ascertain how many townsmen knew for sure that they were the bank robbers and what they looked like.

At the intersections there were just sufficient men alert enough to tie them in with the robbery. A hundred yards down the street a man with a rifle fired after them, and that decided the renegades that discretion was still needed. Even though — minus their green masks — they did not look like bank robbers, nevertheless, they rode and rode hard.

One mile to the east, they turned north at a significant point on the cross trail. That course was maintained for perhaps three hundred yards before they rode around in a loop, first eastward, then southward, and on again to the east. The spot they had chosen to ease up and check over their team and their gear was called Twin Creek. No one lived there, and the name was known only to local people.

Two or three minutes behind at the outset, Jack Brogan turned south at the second intersection. He then continued a block south, then east, then north again. On the way north, a puzzled man pointed after him, and it was borne in upon the young Texan that he was drawing attention to himself by the speed of his riding. So, he slowed down and when he looked back again, others had started to pay attention to him.

Perhaps a bit of bluff would help. He steered the chestnut over to the right side of the street and leaned down to talk to two smokers on a sidewalk bench.

'Which way did they go?' he enquired hoarsely.

One loafer looked absolutely baffled,

but the other had an opinion. He semaphored with his right arm, signalling first north and then east. Jack grinned at him and waved his hat.

'Thanks, amigo, I'll go take a look-see!'

At the next crossing someone fired a rifle. It was probably aimed at his figure, but he went on, ignoring the sudden flurry of interest, and soon he was out of town on the east side and riding towards Twin Creek at a useful speed.

The further he put the town behind him, the more at ease he felt. And his thoughts centred upon the young teller he had been expected to kill, the one who had slipped out of the working area through into the washroom. At the time when he first apprehended the teller, he had been so keyed up, so excited, that the fellow's features had only lightly impinged upon him.

All the time the maximum excitement was being generated in the main part of the building, Jack was thinking that there was something special about the clerk. There *was* something about him. Not just that he was handsome, that his fair beard made him distinguished looking. And behind those thin-rimmed spectacles there was something special about the eyes, too.

He rode with his teeth clenched, breathing in through his mouth. Andy! Andy Miller, of course. Andrew, Sun-up's studious brother. Not Rusty Flood, the adopted son who worked on the ranch, but Andrew who was one year older than himself. The one who ought to be the heir to the Miller holdings, if he could be persuaded to take an interest in the ranch instead of doing bank work away from home. The young man Price had invited him to shoot had been Andy Miller. What an assignment! Orders to shoot his sweetheart's brother. Then, and only then did Jack have an inkling of how far he was out of line with his upbringing.

He was truly shocked. In order to make up for money taken from him by force he had knowingly allied himself with professional outlaws and run the risk of shooting his fellow men for gain.

Why had Will Hobbs allowed him to get in so deep? Will, who had funded him when his spirits were at their lowest ebb. In fact, *where had he been during the critical time?*

Will had not shown up at all, and Bluey had disappeared.

And he, Jack Brogan, second son of the ranching Brogans of San Antonio, was galloping along an unfamiliar trail like a loco maverick with the law somewhere behind and his fellow conspirators somewhere ahead. If they hadn't gone off in another direction, and decided to ditch him. He became very painfully aware that so far no mention at all had been made about his share of the raid proceeds.

What if a posse latched onto him, and the main trio merely dropped out of sight? Now, it seemed the easiest thing in the world to frighten himself. His throat had dried out. He massaged his sticky neck with the white bandanna which had been used to hide his features during the raid. He found himself wondering what it would be like to have a coarse manilla rope draped round his neck in the shape of a noose. He groaned . . .

From somewhere in a dark recess at the back of his mind he recollected that he had muttered the name of the teller shortly after he had struck him. Something like *'stay down, Andy,'* so he must have subconsciously identified the young teller while he was still busy in the bank.

What if Andy had recognised him and used his knowledge to put the local law on his trail? The young teller was certainly well within his rights, but would he do such a thing? Jack thought he would, because he had shown initiative when he slipped out from behind the counter and into the washroom. Out there, on the trail, where dust and heat shimmers mingled, it was hard to visualise the harsh realities of a town being outraged by having its bank robbed.

How long before the pursuit came? *Would* it come? Or would the devious plans of the smartly dressed trio put them all in the clear for one more time?

★　★　★

Thirty minutes later Price and his two partners rode down towards three tall pine trees which looked as if they had been planted by the hand of man, in a straight line. The trees marked the spot where the main stream diverged into two. The first of the twin creeks went away sharply behind the tall pines in a north-easterly direction. However, the second creek which flowed in the same direction was broader, shallower and yet had a larger volume of water. Trees and shrubs grew in lush profusion down the sides of the linked waterways. The land trapped in between the two streams rose in places to nearly one hundred feet, so that a person standing on the banks of one could not see the waters of the other.

Price raised his hand and checked the other two who were following up closely. He gave a yawn, swung out of leather and began to mop himself down. The others did the same.

'Ace, take a look through the spyglass, see if that hombre Brogan is anywhere close.'

Ben Creviss took a drink from his canteen. He surveyed his brown suit which had suffered in the ride at speed from town. It was inevitably marked and creased and he, a fastidious man, did not like it.

'Humbert, I know you don't plan to give this young Texan a cut of the take. So, what do you plan to do with him?'

Price took a swig from a small flat bottle of whisky. Pullar, meanwhile, indicated that their expected visitor was not yet in sight.

'You're the planner,' Creviss prompted, with a shrug of his shoulders.

Pullar fished out three small cigars,

and examined them critically. He handed them out and crackled his own between two fingers and a thumb.

'Well, why don't we get out of sight, shoot him as he comes up an' bury him along with the loot? How would that fill the bill?'

Price made noises suggesting he was in agreement. 'Provided no one else happens along, that would be a useful plan. But the easiest plans are not always the best. Suppose things are not so straight forward back there in town. Perhaps the county sheriff is on a visit to West Flats an' we never knew.

'Maybe we ought to use the Texan to draw any possible pursuit away from us. Yer, that might be the best strategy for us.'

At that point, Pullar reported a single rider coming up fast.

'That'll be him. Now, strip out the saddle rolls, spare clothes, all that gear. Keep within the trees, but put on a bright smile when he gets close. I'll do the talkin'.'

Two minutes later, Brogan approached the trees. He was slightly startled by the speed with which Humbert Price emerged from cover.

'Well howdy, young fellow, you appear to have made good time. No posse on your back trail, either. How's your adrenalin?'

Jack looked baffled. 'No posse that *I* know of. What's adrenalin?'

Price chuckled, and Pullar produced another cigar for the newcomer.

'Did you shoot the teller, like Humbert suggested?' Creviss asked. 'By the way, that adrenalin business. Bert merely wants to know if you were very excited by the proceedings at the bank.'

'It *was* excitin'. I was so keyed up I didn't shoot the teller. Instead, I knocked him unconscious with the barrel of a gun. He passed out. Was that all right?'

Price nodded. He then bent his legs, one at a time, doing an exercise to ease the tiredness in his calves. He finished up by flicking his spur wheels.

'Jack, you did well. But the exercise is not quite over. We want you to take charge of all the horses. Just for a while. Take our three in tow. You said how good you were with cayuses when we first met, didn't you? So, you ride on to the next creek, the further one, that is. Over the ford in the main stream down there a piece, an' take them up the far side.

'Rest them. Rest yourself. Take a bathe. Be alert. We three are goin' to earth down the near side of this creek. For a while, we'll be on constant watch, in case any riders come after us. Now, any questions?'

'Sure,' Jack replied, with a forced smile. 'What will you be doin' if anyone happens along?'

'A good question, young man,' Price acknowledged. He spat out a sliver of tobacco. 'If the visitin' party is small, we'll deal with it. If it's large, we'll be fishin'. An' we'll look like fishermen. Do you approve?'

'You've made no mention of my

share in the loot, Mr Price. Surely that time must be near. You wouldn't be tryin' to put one over on me, in fakin' this fishin', would you?'

Price cackled heartily. 'Double cross on your mind, buddy? We could have shot you, right here at the outset, before you knew we were waitin'. Secondly, we wouldn't be turnin' our mounts over to you if we intended to slip away without leavin' your share. Would we?'

Jack admitted the indisputable logic of Price's argument. As Pullar and Creviss appeared to be growing in nervousness, he took charge of the three spare horses, as had been suggested and went off with them. Ten minutes later, he had crossed the ford and emerged on the far side. Five minutes after that, he found a hollow on the far bank of the second creek, and drove the riding stock down into it. His nerves were still jumping as he stripped off the saddles and blankets, but as soon as he plunged into the water himself he began to feel better.

As he powered his way across the creek on a crawl stroke, his doubts in part returned. If he scrambled out on the west side of the water, he could climb the mound between the creeks and observe the antics of his partners.

14

Nearing the other bank, he slowed up, changed to a breaststroke and began to breathe more deeply. The triangle of upstanding soil trapped between the two streams was heavily grown with sturdy clumps of grasses; dwarf oak and pine trees were interspersed with the grass and fern, and a number of the trees on the highest ground gave the area a crest of sorts.

Jack worked his way out carefully, wondering how the streams of southern Texas were running at that time. He avoided tree roots which stood up from the slippery bank, underwater, and leaned forward to get a purchase on the damp treacherous soil.

Water birds were in abundance, and wild game birds flew out of the undergrowth, perhaps disturbed for the first time by the approach of man. On the slow scramble up the slope to the top of the grade, Jack missed his boots. At first, he was stepping gingerly, wincing when thorns and prickly growths surprised him. The last ten yards were taken with his mouth set grimly and his body tense, as if he was negotiating red hot coals or something very similar.

At the top, he paused for breath with one arm and shoulder resting against an oak bole, and the other arm draped along a branch.

The stream which he could see at the bottom of the downgrade was narrower than the one through which he had swum. The waters appeared to move faster and there was an undercurrent of subdued noise from the deeper parts. Jack blinked, moved his head this way and that. Apart from the water sounds, he could hear voices; the voices of his partners, but they were nowhere to be seen.

Eventually, he made out some sort of natural shelf, more a broad hollow in extent, masked from eyes looking from the east by a thin exquisite line of ferns.

Price, unseen, guffawed with laughter. The other two took up the challenge and made even more noise. Once or twice, they tried to say something but their uncontrollable merriment prevented it.

'Would you believe how green that young Texan is?' Price yelled.

The voice of Creviss took up the challenge, making more noise than Price did, and suggesting that Backmann, Rudy Backmann, his second cousin, had made off with the pay roll belonging to a Brogan herd and gone galloping off south with it to the old squatters' hideout, known to some as Rustlers' Roost.

The substance of what he was saying began to gripe the eavesdropper, but even as Jack realised that he was being duped again, his eyes — blinking away salt sweat and anguish — showed him that he was not the only one to be surprised. There were no signs of fishing, or any sort of preparation for fishing, but the other signs to a trained observer were unmistakable.

Two families of jays, disturbed by encroaching men and horses, fluttered away, squawking and fighting. Higher, and further off, a questing eagle turned an inquisitive eye in the direction of the more westerly stream and checked through the gently moving foliage.

On the extreme southern tip of the timber background, a face showed momentarily. Moving in from the other end, a led horse betrayed a few slight sounds, while from another direction a third sound, that of harness clinking, confirmed that a group of mounted men were closing in upon the three bank robbers who were still engrossed by their own devices.

Jack began to go hot and cold, in spite of the coolness due to his recent swim. Was he visible to the watchers he could not see? Suddenly, he felt as if he were a monument on high ground. It took a conscious effort of will to slowly withdraw altogether behind the tree bole and slide down to earth level.

The unexpected was happening. Pursuers had arrived in force. Price, Pullar and Creviss, who had used him and were discarding him, now were about to receive the one type of confrontation which they were not capable of withstanding. Jack, himself, had to get back the way he had arrived: down the slope, across the second creek and away with all speed.

It was just possible, he supposed, for him to draw the attention of his former partners to the danger creeping up on them, but he had no intention of doing so. They were thieves, tricksters and potential killers. None of them were likable, and he loathed himself for having paid lip service to their way of life. Revenge was different from adopting an alien way of life. Rudy Backmann's cousin, and partners: a trio of back-sliding backstabbing grafters, aiming for a fast buck with no work effort other than a gun threat.

Behind him, he heard a sound. The horses he had left behind him had tired of cropping grass in the green hollow. One of them had plunged into the stream. His heart thumped. Those horses were his way of escape from the fate which attended the Price gang. He needed them to outstrip any pursuit which might come after him. If the same horses made a lot of noise, they would bring about his downfall.

The more he thought about his predicament, the more he felt unsure of himself. Why shouldn't a well organised posse such as this one appeared to be neglect to get in behind their fugitive foes? The descent of the slope was a good deal speedier than the ascent. Every small sound Jack made appeared to him to be magnified. He could no longer hear the animated exchanges from beyond the water.

Breathless, he paused on the brink. Price's big sorrel was the horse first into the water. Pullar's buckskin was poised on the brink of the hollow rim, contemplating an attempt on the descent. Creviss' dun did not appear to be quite so keen on swimming and, fortunately, his own mount was holding back.

He checked his entry into the water long enough to spring up and down a time or two, in a silent effort to dissuade the buckskin from making the leap. It paused, pawing the air with one fore leg, and a slight attack of panic took his attention off it. He dived in, just achieved water deep enough to take him without scraping the treacherous bottom and started back across the stream.

This time, his strokes were not measured, but rushed. All his effort aimed to cut down on time. He swam like a fugitive from a coming explosion. He found himself counting the strokes as he made them, wondering how many more he could make, how much more progress before all hell broke loose behind him. Not being able to hear well with the water in and out of his ears made the suspense a whole lot worse. His breathing became laboured.

The sorrel continued to enjoy its swim, and Jack no longer took note of where it was. There was a plaintive whinneying, and that just preceded the buckskin's ungainly progress into the water.

And then the shooting started. Directly after the first rifle bullet broke the silence, a harsh man's voice issued a challenge. After the briefest of delays, the reply least wanted occurred. All three defenders' rifles replied, firing in different directions.

After that, the whole force of posse riders turned their fire power into the hollow. The noise was very concentrated. The ground vibrated down to the water's edge.

Jack Brogan hurled himself ashore, expecting to be challenged at any second, but no one called out to him and he was allowed to frantically dress himself and keep control of the two remaining horses. The great cacophony of sound must have given him a boost in confidence, because he not only rigged his mount but also the water-shy dun before he realised that two saddles were not altogether necessary.

As he finished his task with the harness, the shooting battle became spasmodic and finally faded out altogether. It was then that he took the two horses by the head and urged them up the slope onto the higher ground. Chance rather than any measured consideration made him mount the dun instead of the tried and trusted chestnut. Clearing the last of the timber screening the hollow, he felt absolutely naked: visible to anyone who cared to look in the right direction.

Replacing the shooting noises were shouts, communications between angry men immersed in the conduct of their duty.

A fine baritone voice called: 'Perkins, you an' Fields, find out where the horses are belongin' to this sorry trio. An' find 'em fast! All the time I don't know, it makes me unhappy. I begin to think we haven't done a thorough job! Me, if I'd just robbed a bank I wouldn't allow my cayuse further away from me than I could spit! So get on with it. Let me know as soon as you have news. Try across the creek. An' what are we all so quiet for? Are we showin' respect for three dead outlaws? Line 'em up on the ground, over there. Go through their pockets, in case they've anythin' to tell us we don't know. Let's go! Pronto!'

Jack Brogan, hearing snatches of all this, turned the head of the dun in the direction he took to be east and rode away. He strained for speed, using his rowels and jerking every now and then at the head rope which guided the chestnut. Soon, he was moving fast, and he no longer bothered about the sounds he was making.

★ ★ ★

Will Hobbs, who had very sensitive hearing, chuckled as he also heard some of County Sheriff Herbert F. Pile's directives to his posse.

Bert Pile was unusually competent as a sheriff. This was probably due to his extensive training with the Pinkerton Detective Agency before he turned his attention to more overt work as a peace officer. On one occasion when the army was missing a lot of money, Pile had been sent along by Pinkertons as an undercover agent to find out what was happening to the army funds. Will Hobbs had accidentally uncovered Pile's cover, but he had kept his knowledge to himself and thereby laid the foundations of a lasting friendship between the two of them.

Hobbs had not lied on that earlier occasion when he had hinted that his face was known to the peace-keeping forces in the area of West Flats. He had known at the time that Bert Pile was the local county sheriff. However, he did not know that Pile was approaching West Flats to act on another matter involving the law when the actual bank raid took place.

Hobbs was still acting in the best interests of the Brogans when he moved in upon Bluey O'Dowell, and forced him to divulge more about the Price gang's future movements than he was supposed to know. Using the information which O'Dowell had divulged, Hobbs had used his influence with Pile to follow the retreating bank robbers in the direction of Twin Creeks. About a furlong short of the screening timber on the west side, Will had slipped away from the posse and found a new location on his own. He had gambled through what O'Dowell had informed him that Price did not intend to give Jack Brogan his cut from the robbery, and he knew there was just a slim chance that Jack would not be close to the other three when the posse sprang its big surprise.

Will had gnawed his nails and offered up a silent prayer as the fusillade of gunfire raked the temporary hideout of the three villains in stores suits.

Hearing that three outlaws were dead and that their horses appeared to be missing had given him confidence that Jack Brogan was not the recipient of the posse's lead. Moreover, if Jack had been segregated and in charge of the horses, there was a fair chance that he was on the far side of the first creek, and — possibly — across the other one.

Presently, Will broke cover, but he kept away from the immediate vicinity of killings and rode in a big loop in the direction of the ford which Jack had used earlier. From cover, he overheard the efforts of the two deputies. Perkins and Fields. Two swimming horses were recovered from the waters of the second creek. Only two out of four. Hobbs' hopes rose again. Before any of the other riders could get across with their mounts he had located the spot where the four horses had been temporarily rested.

He was positively beaming when the shoes of two riding horses, clearly defined on soft ground between trees, revealed a distinctive mark which an observant rider could follow.

★　★　★

Jack Brogan rode hard for over a mile. He had within him the will to put himself a huge distance away from the area where his tricky former allies had paid for their misdeeds. Previously, since he left Texas he had lost a small fortune, he had lost face with the men who had learned to take his orders and to trust him. Now, he did not want to lose his freedom through one single rash act of stupidity performed while he was still depressed through his other losses.

Creviss' dun was an awkward devil, but it soon settled down when it realised that its new rider knew a whole lot of tricks and how to cope with them.

The two horses were moving swiftly along undulating ground. Earth which had at one time been a regular track, but which now was partially grown over. There were patches of scrub, sometimes on one side of the track and sometimes on the other.

Hollows frequently appeared unexpectedly. Sometimes the result of uprooted trees: other times created by large and long gone animals, such as buffalo. The sounds had long since died away, sounds connected with the posse, which had arrived out of nowhere. Nevertheless, Jack turned and looked back from time to time.

Uppermost in his mind, apart from extending the distance between himself and those who might seek him, was the urge to get down into a valley of some sort, so that anyone distantly behind him would not at once locate him through a spyglass.

Unbeknown to him, at first, a problem was creeping up on him. A problem of his own making. He had rushed the job of rigging his mounts for riding. As a result, the fixing of the saddles had been less than efficient. The saddle on the back of Creviss' dun was not the one the stocky little fellow had used habitually. Slowly, imperceptibly, the blanket and saddle under Jack began to move. He soon realised what he had done, but he declined to dismount and make the necessary adjustments until he had reached a distant landmark which he hoped was the start of a downgrade.

He was still full of riding confidence when the dun gave a whinny which sounded more to be through annoyance than pleasure. At once, the horse bucked, sidekicked and danced jerkily on its forelegs. On account of the slack fitting blanket and saddle, Jack failed to adjust sufficiently to keep his balance. He found himself flying through the air like a frog. His braced forearms were not sufficient to break his fall. He landed heavily, cracked his head on an eroded rock and lay still.

* * *

'Jack, are you goin' to sleep forever?'

The voice was the soft, silky one

belonging to Will Hobbs. The hands which supported his head and held the water canteen to Jack's lips were hard, sinewy and calloused in places, but they were doing a very welcome job and assuring the bruised discomfited young Texan that he was still in the land of the living with at least one friend and ally.

'Will, what happened? No, don't bother to answer that. Tell me somethin' else, instead. How come you got here when most of the action was over? How come you knew where to look for me?'

Hobbs chuckled rather drily. 'You surely do have the devil's own luck, young fellow. You were thrown by a dun horse. One you didn't quite saddle properly. Probably because you were in an awful hurry to get away from the spot where County Sheriff Herbert F. Pile was eliminating the three known outlaws who robbed the West Flats bank.'

Jack nodded, eyes closed, and attempted to support himself. Will placed him against a rock. He opened his eyes, but the late afternoon sun proved very searching, so that he had to close them again. Jack's stomach lurched. He felt anything but healthy, and yet his questing mind was seeking to know of his immediate predicament.

'I guess you're goin' to tell me you've known Sheriff Pile from way back, an' that you've arranged for him to go back to town without botherin' to come lookin' for any fourth member of the outlaw team?'

'For a jasper who ought to be sufferin' with chronic concussion you figure things real well, young Brogan. I said you were lucky. Pile has ridden back to town with the three dead bodies. What he doesn't have with him is the loot from the bank. So, when the rewards are considered President Stanley T. Brewsford will be hangin' on to his ten per cent.'

Hobbs abandoned his charge for a short while, moving a few yards to check the contents of the saddle which had been loosely on the back of the troublesome dun horse. While he was away, Jack became aware that the chestnut was also within calling distance. He marvelled that so much had gone right since his senses left him.

Hobbs called out to him from the tiny park, where the two runaway horses and his own were resting.

'You got wind of the posse's arrival, Jack. So you got back out of the water with all speed, saddled two horses in a blindin' hurry an' caused yourself a whole lot of trouble. The blanket you used for the dun had two or three burrs stuck in it. At first, I guess, they didn't bother the animal because they weren't pressed into its hide. After a while, though, the blanket shifted an' the burrs drove home an' hurt it, an' then it went wild. Threw you when you weren't expectin' trouble. So that about explains how you landed in a heap like you did, instead of bein' two or three miles away, further east.'

Jack whistled in disbelief. He rose slowly to his feet, and gingerly tried his hat this way and that, attempting to wear it in such a way that the bump on his head would not be in close contact with the material. He partially succeeded.

As Will came back, Jack remarked: 'You should have been a detective in the army, not a pony soldier, Will.'

Will beamed, temporarily ironing out most of the lines in his weathered face. 'Oh, I don't know, Jack. I was lucky when you picked a horse to ride which had a special mark on one of its shoes. But with the dust you were puttin' up I'd have found you, in any case. By the way, did you give any thought to what I said about the bank money?'

Jack stood rocking backwards and forwards, his hands on his hips. 'What exactly did you have in mind, amigo? You must know by now that *I* don't have any loot money with me!'

Will strolled up and stood directly in front of Jack, also with his hands on his hips. 'I was thinkin' that you an' me, we might locate the money, which is very likely not far from here. I think this whole affair has given you an almighty shock. You're no two-bit outlaw. Here you are with a chance to regain your self esteem. You could return the loot, if we found it, an' maybe recoup some of your earlier losses when the payroll was heisted.'

Jack thought hard about these interesting suggestions. At first, his brown stubbled face showed hope and a lot of animation, but gradually his expression changed.

'There's something you don't know, Will. In that bank, Sun-up's brother, Andrew Miller, was one of the tellers. I had to hit him with my gun to render him unconscious. Otherwise . . . '

It was Hobbs' turn to frown with speculation. At length, he came up with an answer. 'Well, you could have shot him, which would have been worse. Back home in Texas, did you have much to do with this Andrew before he came north?'

Jack shrugged. 'Not really. He acted

older than me. Besides, he was studious. The only thing the two of us had in common was a feelin' that we didn't want to be cow nurses all our lives.'

Will agreed with Jack that it would be one hell of a situation if Dawn Miller's brother was to give evidence which could send him to the penitentiary.

Nevertheless, the two of them mounted up and backtracked to the scene of the recent shoot-out after partaking of a makeshift campfire meal. There was no harm in looking for the spot where the loot might be buried.

15

After a half hour's search, the two determined young men found the leather money hold-alls buried at a depth of three feet between the roots of a large oak-type tree at the rear of the spot where Price and his two sidekicks had gone to earth. By the time the bags were unearthed, the diggers were tired and weak through lack of perspiration, and only the great interest which large sums of money engender — even in those who do not love the stuff — kept them from becoming violently argumentative about the exact amount.

'All right, let's say we have about thirty thousand dollars, Jack,' Will remarked, waving a small cigar in Brogan's direction. 'Price an' his boys wouldn't have time to count it all, either. It's a lot of money. No one knows we have it. If you took it, not havin' anyone to share it with who took part in the raid, you could return home with a handsome profit. More than Backmann an' company took from you. What do you say?'

Jack's grin was a bit forced. 'It ain't all that simple, is it? See here, Will, you've happened along twice now when I was almost done for. How do you see the outcome? I'm askin' for advice.'

'If you take the money, you'll have to disappear, won't you? In case anyone finds out where the loot ended up. If you didn't dare to return the cash, on account of Andy Miller, the teller, that would be something else. I could take it in myself, an' turn over the reward money percentage to you later. But that way, you'd always have to live with doubts, an' that wouldn't be easy. Not for a young fellow with a lot of years ahead of him. Let's the two of us take in the money an' play it from there. What do you say?'

'All right, Will, if that's the way you see it, we'll take in the cash together.

Even if it costs me a year or two in the pen for complicity. Only not tonight, huh? We're both tired an' we've had a busy day.'

Will shook his head doggedly. 'Let's see it through today, Jack, while we have our thoughts in order. If the worst comes to the worst, I can always tell a few lies about where you were when the bank was bein' robbed. Let's get the issue settled, once an' for all.'

Without enthusiasm, Jack agreed.

★   ★   ★

Towards seven o'clock in the evening the two riders approached the bank. Both of them had shaved and brushed their clothing. Jack had exchanged his bright shirt and bandanna for a white shirt and a string tie. As soon as they angled their mounts for the nearest streetside hitchrail, the led dun with the leather hold-alls strapped to its otherwise empty saddle began to attract attention.

A constable with a long face and lean jaw looked a bit shaken as they walked across to him and asked permission to see the bank president on a matter of great importance. The constable glanced behind him at the boarded up windows, blinked a lot and finally agreed to take their message indoors.

Eventually, they were admitted. Jack took with him two hold-alls, while Will carried the third. Bert Jakes, the older teller, had gone home. The broken glass had been swept up and the working area cleared. Andrew Miller answered a polite knock on the private door, and after a brief chat with the constable the two visitors were ushered in. Young Miller had a light bandage round his head and a speculative look behind his spectacles. Brewsford, the president, was seated behind the big desk. He reached for his ear trumpet as Will explained their business.

'Good day to you, Mr Brewsford. I'm Will Hobbs, from San Antonio, Texas. My friend is from the same place. Meet

Jack Brogan, member of a ranchin' family.'

One by one, they shook hands with the old man, while Andrew Miller cleared his throat a time or two. 'Mr Brewsford, you may recall I, too, am from San Antonio. Mr Brogan and I have met before.'

Jack and Andrew shook hands, rather formally. Jack glanced at Andrew's bandaged head. He coloured up slightly. Andrew's expression did not give anything away. In the background, the old man suddenly exploded with interest.

'You've recovered *my* bank funds? Incredible! Scarcely possible. Perhaps you'll be good enough to sit down an' convince me.'

Will outlined their having found a runaway horse and the hold-alls having turned up in a hollow in the Twin Creek area where they had planned to spend the night fishing. Andrew was brought back into the action to count the money. When the story was told and the president was convinced that all his money was back on his desk, Andrew cleared his throat and gave the total.

'Thirty thousand one hundred and seven dollars, Mr Brewsford. The reward percentage will therefore be just over three thousand dollars. I think our visitors are to be congratulated, don't you?'

'Well, er, yes, I guess that is so.' Brewsford did not sound altogether happy about finally parting with the reward money. He was blinking hard as he went on. 'The sheriff only had three bodies for us to inspect. There's a fourth hombre somewheres, not accounted for.'

'But you're payin' the reward for the return of your money, Mr Brewsford,' Andrew reminded him. 'Surely these two respectable gents require only our thanks an' gratitude, if we are to maintain our goodwill efforts with the public. Mr Brogan will want to get back to his ranch in Texas. He may even be contemplatin' becomin' my brother-in-law quite soon. Isn't that so, Jack?'

Andrew had cunningly turned his attention to Jack, who willingly confirmed what the young teller had in mind. 'Why certainly, a weddin' is a distinct possibility, Andrew. I almost proposed before I came north. There's just a bit of unfinished trail business to be taken care of an' then we'll be on our way. Tomorrow, however, would be time enough for a settlement with Mr Brewsford.'

The business came to a head without further delays. The reward money was heaped into one hold-all, and put aside ready to be collected by the recipients at a mutually convenient hour the following morning. The sensational news spread rapidly round the town. Jack and Will stayed in the best suite at the local hotel, and partook of dinner with Andrew, who was anxious for news from home, as well as other discreet details about matters more recent.

Andrew learned how the payroll was lost, and Will had it confirmed during the conversation that his partner intended to seek out and confound Rudy Backmann and the three desperadoes who had all but killed him when the payroll was stolen.

★   ★   ★

The following morning, Jack and Will left early to avoid a lot of publicity. Will had accepted as his part of the reward money the cash he had advanced on a previous occasion to pay off the Circle B trail drovers. He rejected any further cash, and would not discuss the matter further. Andrew rode with them for about a mile out of town, then he returned and the two went on alone.

For the return to Texas, they were using a route which was a few miles to westward of the one taken by the herd on the way north. On the second day, they moved eastward and studied the dust put up by another herd, probably a bigger one than the Circle B. They talked with two riders scouring the left flank for stragglers and had it confirmed to them that the ghost town associated with rustlers was another day's ride further south and that rustling attempts had been made on two occasions.

By mid-morning on the third day they had their first glimpse of the abandoned town which now bore the appellation of Rustlers' Roost. From the flat top of a shallow mesa they looked down on it through a spyglass. While they were studying the distant ramshackle buildings, a party of five riders left the settlement from the far end and rode out towards the east.

'We can't tell how many groups will be usin' that town at any one time, Jack,' Will pointed out calmly. 'One thing seems significant, though, they don't appear to have any cattle strewn about.'

'I'm glad you noticed that, Will,' Jack replied calmly. 'We don't want innocent cattle to suffer when we go into action.'

Will turned on his partner in

surprise. At this juncture, he was expecting a possible change of mind, but Jack seemed even more determined than before.

'Too bad those riders were so far away. Too far to identify,' the ex-soldier mused.

Jack shook his head dourly. 'I know for certain Backmann, Thompson, Dupont an' McNye weren't among those five, amigo. Even at that distance, little mannerisms show in the way a man rides. Don't forget I've studied them all. There'll be no mistakes in the next clash. I'm goin' to fight, an' fight dirty, the way they're used to.'

While Will mulled over Jack's last deliberations, the latter held up a wet finger and patiently measured the slight breeze which was blowing from north to south.

After that, Jack turned his attention to the intervening ground between the mesa and the nearest buildings of Rustlers' Roost. He became quite animated about a huge triangle of scrubland which had a long boundary encroaching along the northern side of the peeling buildings.

'I don't want to rush you, amigo, but I'm all anxious to get down to that patch of scrub before the wind changes or fades out on us. What do you say about carryin' the action to the enemy as soon as we can get within striking distance?'

Will rolled onto his back, his hat pushed back off his forehead and his neck supported by his linked hands. 'Action, action, action. That's all you ever think about, Brogan. An' here am I, freshly out of the army an' lookin' forward to a quiet, uneventful life. You won't take any notice of me, but workin' through a town, lookin' for fugitives calls for a special kind of skill. Special experience, if you like. A short lapse of vigilance, no more than a couple of seconds an' the man on the prowl gets winged.

'It could take a long time for the two of us to catch your four enemies unawares in all those buildings, even if we maintained the element of surprise all the way. There could be sixty buildings, more or less, down there. How shall we know where to look without putting ourselves at risk?'

Jack finally collapsed the spyglass, rolled over and grinned.

'Quite a speech, amigo. Quite a speech. But I think I know where to find a jasper like Backmann. He'll be in the best room at the best hotel. Or, failin' that, he'll have set up quarters in the bank! How's that for figurin'?'

Will shifted easily, and pointed his trigger fingers to add weight to his argument. 'Even so, young Brogan, we have to *find* the best hotel, and the bank. We have to win time to infiltrate that far. Have you considered the time factor?'

Jack hauled his Winchester closer and began to check it over. Will awaited his answer. He grinned.

'The time factor won't affect us too much. Not if we panic them first.

Shouldn't you be givin' attention to your hardware? I'm surprised the army didn't make you finicky in such matters.'

★ ★ ★

An approach unseen to the huge triangle of scrub took more than half an hour. As they moved closer, so the slight breeze freshened and maintained its direction, north to south. Will was not very surprised when Jack produced matches and intimated that he intended to smoke out the villains, burn the ghost town to the ground, if necessary.

It occurred to Will that a whole lot of Circle B money might still be stached away within the bounds of the ghost town. Paper money, too. Money which could be destroyed in next to no time by fire. And his partner did not appear to be greatly concerned about winning it back, or losing it.

'Ready to go, amigo?' Jack asked. He was on his knees, ready to apply the first match to tinder dry grass and scrub. Will had the reins of their two horses over his arm. He took a drink from his canteen, and nodded. 'Ready to go, amigo.'

The match flared. The grass caught fire. No further matches were required. A few touches here and there with a burning brand were enough to exploit the sizzling scrub and to send the first billowing wave of smoke eddying towards the town.

* * *

At first, the men who were in the town paid little attention to the advancing menace. Apart from the five riders who had gone out earlier there were only four, and those four were the men on Jack Brogan's elimination list. They were the men in funds and they did not have to go out making risky raids while they had money to spend and plenty of rations to hand.

Rudolph Backmann had always had a

hankering for the soft life. Clean shirts, soft upholstery, a fine bed and the very best of food and drink. He was slow to pick up the roaring noise caused by the burning of the buildings at the north end of town. The smoke did not offend his nostrils because he was relaxing in a deep bath of water on the first floor of the hotel with a big lighted cigar between his lips.

His mates had gone off to their favourite quarters, in the bank, to play a few hands at poker before considering what they wanted for lunch. Entirely by coincidence, the riding horses were in the stable at the south end of town and, so far, the smell of smoke had not panicked them.

Backmann tossed aside a foam-flecked magazine, reflected that his bath water was getting cold and found that the two tall jugs he was depending upon for supplies were almost empty. Cursing to himself, he drank two fingers of whisky from a glass, and decided to be patient for a while longer. He put his head back, resting it against the raised portion of the large portable bath, and dozed.

His last thought as he slipped off into a shallow sleep was that Rustlers' Roost was not complete. It did not have any willing ladies to round out a riding man's essential needs. What a pity it was so costly to transport extra people for entertainment and service.

An inch of cigar smoke fell on his chest, just above the water level. It sizzled on his damp skin, startled him into wakefulness and caused him to lose the butt of the cigar in the water. His temper gave out. He knocked over one of the empty jugs, which shattered. Next, he hefted up a six-gun and aimed it over his shoulder, firing backwards to hit the window beyond the bath. The glass shattered about the bullet hole. He frowned as the gunshot sound boomed in his ears in the enclosed space.

He filled his lungs and shouted.

'Hey, you three ornery jaspers, get

along here an' bring me some hot water! I'm freezin'! You hear me, Thompson? Frenchy! Burro! I want action right now!'

By that time, the line of burning buildings in which the hotel stood was exuding flame and smoke, and filling the upper atmosphere with ash. Two buildings away, an office block was just beginning to catch fire. Suddenly, another bullet went through the shattered window glass. This time fired from outside. Splinters of glass flew all around the bath and the man who was in the process of getting out of it.

'Backmann! It's time to come out here an' show how good you are with a gun! If you don't hurry, the water in your bath will boil under you! An' don't forget I'm waitin' either!'

Backmann knew the voice. He was startled on two counts. Firstly, he was staggered by the fire and its progress towards the hotel. Secondly, Jack Brogan's voice was like an avenger from the grave. Brogan ought to have died many days before, shortly after the payroll was heisted.

'Who's that callin' the odds?'

'It's me, Jack Brogan! You know the voice! I'll give you a minute! Get your pants on an' bring your gun!'

By this time, Rudy Backmann knew the score. Brogan had survived and he was man enough to enter this ghost town and demand a gun showdown. Backmann partially dried himself in a silent fury, his fingers wet and too smooth to do a swift job. Still not properly dried, he pulled on his pants, struggled into his shirt and hastily buckled on his gun belt. All the time he was busy, his thoughts were weighing his chances. He had to come out as Brogan had suggested; any sort of circuitous route would put him into the face of the fire. His eyes would water with the smoke and the advantage would go to the challenger.

Judging by his voice, Brogan was down the street a piece. Thompson and the other two were down that way. The bank was fifty yards from the hotel. If they were not drunk, there was a possibility that they would be in a position to nullify any advantage which Brogan had. They could sneak up behind him and gun him down from the rear. If only they were fully alert. But Backmann had his doubts about them. They should have known about this fast-moving fire. They should have been along to warn him, long before this.

'All right, Brogan, I'm comin' out! Hit the road. I'll be with you right away!'

'As soon as you hit the dirt, Rudy, I'll show you where I am!'

And that was the order of events. Backmann leapt into the street from the hotel foyer, dabbing his eyes against the wreaths of smoke, and turning his back on the tongues of fire, so very close. Jack Brogan then leapt into view from the other side of the street, thirty-five yards further down.

'Make your draw, Rudy! If you delay,

the fire will have you before I do!'

Brogan was too darned confident, damn him. Where were the others, the back-up team? A rifle fired from the west side of the street. It was fired at some target in the bank area. So, it was not one of the trio. Brogan was not alone. The young Texan flinched at the sound of the shot, but he did not take his gaze from Backmann.

'You lived dirty, Backmann, but you're goin' to die clean!'

The taunt shook the former trail boss quite a bit. Temper made him go for the draw before he had his hands fully under control. He had two guns, one on each hip. In an effort to disconcert his adversary, he pulled his left hand gun and went down on his left knee. Jack drew his one right handed Colt, and fired accurately. His first bullet was away a second before Backmann's but due to the other's tactics it flew an inch or so too high.

Backmann's first shot passed so close to Jack's ear that his head was filled with a buzzing noise. Down went Jack, throwing himself forward and balancing the .45 on both elbows. Backmann missed him again. Jack's second shot put flying dirt in the outlaw's face, and the third struck just to the left of the breastbone as he cleared the dust from his eyes.

Backmann lurched on his knee, lost his balance and slipped sideways into the dirt, getting off another bullet at a peculiar angle, and then he was folding up, already dead.

The staccato sounds of the shooting exchanges had penetrated the whole town, in spite of the roar put up by burning timber. Instinct made Jack dive for shelter on the east side. At once, he worked his way nearer the bank, at the same time thumbing bullets into his empty chambers.

Backmann was dead, but all the other men involved in the shooting affray were busy. Two men erupted through the back door of the bank and ran furiously further up the street. Will

Hobbs was not sure how far Jack had progressed up the street since he plunged into cover. In an effort to put himself into a superior position, Will came out of the office at ground level opposite the bank. He ran up a flight of wooden steps to the next floor, taking them two at a time. As it was an external flight, he was taking a calculated risk. At the top, a balk of timber was holding open a trapdoor which gave access to a narrow balcony.

Directly opposite, the one outlaw who had stayed in the bank was anxiously peering through a narrow gun port in the front door. His cheek pressed against the stock of his rifle as he studied the scene opposite. Hobbs was half way up the flight of wooden stairs when Frenchy recovered sufficiently to loose off a rifle bullet at him.

In effect, the bullet missed its human target, but it struck the supporting timber and allowed the trapdoor to fall just as Hobbs' head and shoulders were due to go through it. Dupont scarcely believed what he had done. Even though he had missed his target, Hobbs came back down the stairs in an untidy backward somersault, landing at the bottom in a crumpled heap. He stayed still.

Within seconds, Jack Brogan entered the building through the back window. He kicked open the door to the front office and dived through it, sailing along the polished floor with his arms spread and his gun held clear. There was gun smoke in the room and instinct at once told him he was not alone. There was movement. Overhead, three leather money pouches were slung over a central beam. They were crammed full and fastened.

Money. Paper money. Probably it constituted the payroll for the Brogan herd. Jack was doubly interested. It meant — if he was right — that the family funds were not all spent. Furthermore, greedy outlaws would not leave a burning town without making an effort to take their loot with them . . .

Jack crawled behind the settee, decided it was substantial enough to withstand a few bullets, and was inclined to take a risk. He whistled a few bars of Dixie, and waited. Dupont's patience gave out. He rolled clear of the flap entrance to the rear of the counter, panning his rifle as he did so. Two bullets missed to one side of the settee, and the third entered and carried on, into the wall.

Jack rolled clear of the other end and hit Frenchy in the head with his first shot. The French-Canadian lowered his head to the shiny surface and expired.

Once again, Jack began to wonder where Will had positioned himself, but this time he was quite willing to take on all the action alone. The memory of Frenchy's high pitched voice impinged upon his thoughts. He rolled to his feet, stepped over to the front door and peered through the shooting slot. The sight of Will in a crumpled heap right opposite gave him a nasty jolt of surprise, but it also stiffened his resolve to out-think and outshoot these three desperadoes who had left him for dead not so very long ago.

Not knowing whether Will Hobbs was alive or dead, he nevertheless put his ruthless plan into action. A minute or two of concentration assured him that he could imitate the dead Canadian's voice. He smiled to himself rather grimly. Frenchy's rifle was easily long enough to hook down the three money pouches. One after another, he knocked them to the floor.

Next, he kicked them over towards the main door. A quick glance through the slot assured him that no one was sneaking up on him. Taking a deep breath, he opened one side.

After staring hard at the corpse, he closed his eyes and shouted, putting a lot of effort into his high-pitched effort.

'Hey, Burro, Link! What's keepin' you, for goodness' sake? The action is over! Backmann is dead! I've just salivated Brogan, an' that's the lot! Will you get down here an' help me remove this money? Hell, all these notes are goin' to go up in smoke if we ain't careful! And there's only three of us to share it!'

At first, all he could hear when he stopped shouting was the ominous roar of burning wood, but soon the two cautious outlaws caught on. The lure of money had convinced them that all was well. To further the charade, Jack tossed the bags, one at a time, out into the middle of the street where they landed in a close dusty heap.

Link Thompson and Burro McNye emerged slowly, at first. Then, as if attempting to outdo one another, they chased down the dirt surface holding their weapons wide and squinting in the smoke-laden atmosphere.

Jack closed the door, glanced over Dupont's rifle, and carefully poked the muzzle through the slot. The outlaws arrived in a rush. Briefly, they glanced at Hobbs' still figure and then they turned their attention to the door of the bank. Instinct told them something was amiss. Closer observation revealed the dark business end of the rifle. The targets stiffened.

Thompson, who was pointing, absorbed the first bullet. The impact, as it ripped into his chest knocked him backwards, and Burro was put off balance at the same time. Dupont's last bullet hit McNye under the left arm as he attempted to turn away, too late. The two outlaws made a macabre tableau, draped untidily in the dirt as if guarding the money bags.

Will Hobbs stirred as Jack hurried across to him. His head had suffered. So had one knee and the ankle on the other side. Will started to shake his head, but his senses started to swim again. He seated himself on the steps and put his head between his knees.

'You all right, Will?'

'Sure, I'm all right. Can't a fellow get a bit of rest now an' again without all this noise? Brogan you're gettin' too handy with guns for my likin' an' what's more you don't need me to back you up any more. Besides, this ole town is gettin' too hot for me. Know what? I reckon I'll head for home. How about joinin' me?'

Jack steadied Will as he rose to his feet again. They gripped one another by the shoulders and then thought about leaving.

16

Will Hobbs frowned and stared, and remarked: 'What in tarnation is this? It says 'Sun-up loves Jack.' Now who in the world is Sun-up, do you suppose?'

The heart was carved out of the bark of the northernmost tree on the west side of the bathing creek near the Brogan ranch. An arrow pierced the heart, and the words were only just decipherable, due to the undulations in the bark.

A yard away, Jack Brogan shrugged and grinned, and fingered his stubbled chin. His chestnut horse flicked its tail and rolled its neck encouragingly.

'Oh, I don't know. Might have something to do with that Miller girl I used to know. Which reminds me. I have to see her father about something special. Unfinished business to do with the Brogans and the Millers.'

The water looked tempting, but in spite of the long monotonous ride back into south Texas, Jack felt nervous, jumpy even. For umpteen nights he had dreamed of the reunion with his girl, Sun-up. Now, his mind was full of doubts. Maybe she had not waited. Maybe she would have tired of him and his off-putting ways. She might even have developed a crush on his older brother, Roary.

'Say, Jack, you're actin' kind of funny. Didn't you say you were cravin' for a swim in this particular creek?'

'Yer, I did, Will, but I figure I ought to get back home first. The folks will be anxious, an' I haven't seen my brother, Roary, since he came home! So maybe it would be best to put off the swim till later.'

Will nodded and accepted Jack's notions. Side by side, they rode down the side of the creek. Some fifty yards further on, their horses began to show signs of interest, the sort of interest engendered by other animals of the same species. Even so, the familiar grey mare, the mount of Dawn Miller, took the two riders by surprise.

Suddenly they pulled up and peered around.

A gentle female voice called to them from the direction of the water's edge. 'If that's you, Jack Brogan, an' you're finally ready to make that overdue announcement, I'd like to be there when you do it. Will you wait till I get dressed?'

Her face looked rounder on account of her long auburn hair being flattened and shaped by the water. Only her head was showing, but she looked fresh, anxious and full of love.

'When you hear some of the things I've been up to, maybe you won't be quite so keen to go through with our engagement, Sun-up! But it surely is me, Jack, the would-be drover an' trail boss. In the flesh. Back to you an' San Antone, if that's the way you want it!'

Will cleared his throat, politely

pointed out that he too was in a hurry. 'You two must have a whole lot of catchin' up to do. So why don't I ride ahead to the ranch, take the proceeds of the sale with me, an' alert the folks to what lies in store for them?'

Dawn approved. She stayed down in the water until her big bathing towel was handed to her. Will moved on, and such was the magnetism between the young couple that his exit was scarcely noticed. Jack helped dry Dawn's hair. He started to unburden himself.

'Your Uncle Matt isn't comin' back, Sun-up. We lost him at a river crossin' a long way from here. He was like my uncle, as well as yours.'

'Some of the boys are back. We heard about Matt's demise, an' some other hard times you had. Welcome back, trail boss. You've grown up. It shows in your face, in the way you talk. Consideration for others. I no longer have any doubts about you. Escort me back to the ranch, why don't you? You've been missed.'

After a long, warm, healing embrace, Jack boosted his girl into the saddle. He mounted and rode along beside her. His protracted self-imposed work trial was over.

THE END

We do hope that you have enjoyed reading this large print book.

Did you know that all of our titles are available for purchase?

We publish a wide range of high quality large print books including:
Romances, Mysteries, Classics
General Fiction
Non Fiction and Westerns

Special interest titles available in large print are:
The Little Oxford Dictionary
Music Book, Song Book
Hymn Book, Service Book

Also available from us courtesy of Oxford University Press:
Young Readers' Dictionary
(large print edition)
Young Readers' Thesaurus
(large print edition)

For further information or a free brochure, please contact us at:
Ulverscroft Large Print Books Ltd.,
The Green, Bradgate Road, Anstey,
Leicester, LE7 7FU, England.
Tel: (00 44) **0116 236 4325**
Fax: (00 44) **0116 234 0205**

DEAD IS FOR EVER

Amy Sadler

After rescuing Hope Bennett from the clutches of two trailbums, Sam Carver made a serious mistake. He killed one of the outlaws, and reckoned on collecting the bounty on Lew Daggett. But catching Sam off-guard, Daggett made off with the girl, leaving Sam for dead. However, he was only grazed and once he came to, he set out in search of Hope. When he eventually found her, he was forced into a dramatic showdown with his life on the line.

SMOKING STAR

B. J. Holmes

In the one-horse town of Medicine Bluff two men were dead. Sheriff Jack Starr didn't need the badge on his chest to spur him into tracking the killer. He had his own reason for seeking justice, a reason no-one knew. It drove him to take a journey into the past where he was to discover something else that was to add even greater urgency to the situation — to stop Montana's rivers running red with blood.

THE WIND WAGON

Troy Howard

Sheriff Al Corning was as tough as they came and with his four seasoned deputies he kept the peace in Laramie — at least until the squatters came. To fend off starvation, the settlers took some cattle off the cowmen, including Jonas Lefler. A hard, unforgiving man, Lefler retaliated with lynchings. Things got worse when one of the squatters revealed he was a former Texas lawman — and no mean shooter. Could Sheriff Corning prevent further bloodshed?

BLACK RIVER

Adam Wright

John Dyer has come to the insignificant little town of Black River to destroy the last living reminder of his dark past. He has come to kill. Jack Hart is determined to stop him. Only he knows the terrible truth that has driven Dyer here, and he knows that only he can beat Dyer in a gunfight. Ex-lawman Brad Harris is after Dyer too — to avenge his family. The stage is set for madness, death and vengeance.